Eventer's Dream

D1312978

Eventer's Dream

Caroline Akrill

ARMADA

For Lizzie
in memory of some very similar vases

Eventer's Dream was first published in the U.K. in 1981
by Arlington Books, and republished in Dragon in 1984
This Armada edition was first published in 1990
This impression 1991

Armada is an imprint of
HarperCollins Children's Books, part of
HarperCollins Publishers Ltd,
77–85 Fulham Palace Road,
Hammersmith, London W6 8JB

Copyright © Caroline Akrill 1983

Set in Times

Printed and bound in Great Britain by
HarperCollins Book Manufacturing, Glasgow

CONTENTS

1

Uncertain Advantages

"The thing is," Nigella said, giving the teapot a vigorous shake, "that if you *did* decide to come and help us out, we couldn't pay you much."

"Hardly anything at all, really," Henrietta said. "Just pocket money wages. But on the other hand, there would be certain advantages."

I sat beside the stone-cold Aga in the antiquated kitchen and I thought of the pot-holes in the drive. I remembered the straggling laurel bushes that bordered it, smelling of damp and leaf-mould and fox. The broken park railings. The dead elms. The grim old house with its blind and shuttered windows and the heavy atmosphere of age and neglect and decay.

"Certain advantages for whom?" I enquired. I couldn't imagine that they could possibly be for me.

"For us, naturally," Henrietta said. "Because we would have someone to organize the stables. And for you Elaine, because you would have a job, and somewhere to live, and a stable and keep for your horse."

"I haven't got a horse," I said.

"Oh, but you will have," Henrietta said confidently. "I mean, if you want to go eventing, you will need a horse to do it on. Unless," she added in an uncertain tone, "you were thinking of using one of ours?"

"Oh, no," I said. "That wouldn't do at all."

In actual fact, it was exactly what I had in mind. The truth of the matter was that I couldn't possibly afford to buy a horse of my own and I planned to find myself a sponsor in the shape of a sympathetic employer, who would provide me with a mount and a chance to compete. So far though, I had drawn a blank. This was my fifteenth interview and already I was planning my escape.

Henrietta looked relieved. "I'm glad," she said. "Eventing can be a bit risky and horses are so expensive these days. One just can't afford to keep breaking legs and things."

"Quite," I said.

I wondered why I had accepted the invitation to tea in such unpromising circumstances, when the situation was so clearly hopeless. Any sensible person, confronted with a pair of prospective employers like Nigella and Henrietta in their skintight jeans, their out-at-the-elbow anoraks and their cut down wellingtons, all liberally coated with horse hairs and mud, would have fled the place on sight.

Nigella squinted down the spout of the teapot. Her long dark plait was speckled with hay seeds and tied at the end with bailer twine. When she had tried to pour the tea, nothing had come out. She poked a ball point pen energetically up and down the spout. "I don't suppose eventing is any more risky than any other equestrian activity," she commented, "provided that horse and rider are properly prepared." After a bit of fishing about inside the pot, she managed to flip a sodden brown lump on to the table. She splashed tea into three chipped red beakers. We helped ourselves to milk from a bottle and

8

damp sugar straight out of a packet. "Sorry it's a bit informal," Nigella said.

Henrietta looked round the kitchen in a vague sort of way. "There *were* some biscuits," she said. I wondered how long ago there had been biscuits. Last week perhaps, or last month. There certainly didn't seem to be any today.

"Can you cook?" Nigella said suddenly. "I mean, nothing too special, not cordon bleu or anything like that. Just cakes and puddings and pies and things."

"And biscuits," Henrietta added. "We like biscuits."

I swallowed a mouthful of musty tasting tea. I was prepared for this. After all, I was an experienced interviewee by now and I had discovered that people who advertised for help with horses often wanted anything from a gardener to a children's nanny and merely offered the horses as bait.

"The advertisement didn't mention cooking," I said firmly. "It just said, 'Help wanted in small, friendly, private stable'."

"Ah," Henrietta said, looking guilty. "So we did say private. We thought we might have."

"You mean it isn't?" I said, surprised.

"Not exactly," Henrietta said. She stared at the tea bag. Her wild mane of auburn hair flowed over her shoulders and on to the table. It was full of knots and it looked as if it hadn't been combed for months.

"We do take the odd livery," Nigella admitted. "Well, perhaps rather more than the odd one."

"And we do let out horses for hunting now and then," Henrietta said. "Well, perhaps more often than not."

"In that case you are not a private stable at all," I

9

said. "You are a commercial enterprise. You are running a business."

"Only in a manner of speaking," Nigella said. "And not out of choice. We are not motivated by profit. We only do it to live."

"We wouldn't dream of doing it if we didn't have to," Henrietta said in a defensive tone. She picked up the ball point pen and poked at the tea bag. "Having to earn a living is the most frightful bore."

"But in your advertisement you distinctly said it was a private stable," I reminded them. "It just isn't true." I pulled the page torn from *Horse and Hound* out of my pocket and spread it on the table. The advertisement was ringed with red crayon. "Small, friendly, private stable . . ."

"I wish you wouldn't keep *on* about it," Henrietta said. "It isn't as if it really matters." She rolled the tea bag over and leaned closer to it, narrowing her eyes.

"We *are* friendly," Nigella said.

"You are not private," I said.

"We *are* small," Nigella argued. "That's two out of three."

"It's still misleading," I said, "and also illegal. You can't say things that aren't true in an advertisement. You could be prosecuted under the Trades Descriptions Act. It's misrepresentation."

"Heavens," Nigella said. "How awful. I had no idea."

"This tea bag," Henrietta commented, "isn't a tea bag at all."

"What else did we say in the advertisement?" Nigella scanned the page, interested.

"It's a mouse."

10

We transferred our attention to the tea bag. It was definitely a mouse; very small, very saturated, and very dead. Nigella clapped her hand over her mouth and let out a low moan.

"If it's any consolation," Henrietta said, "I should think it was practically sterilized by the boiling water." She lifted the mouse up with the ball point pen and plopped it down on the advertisement. Nigella watched, appalled, as she wrapped it into a neat parcel.

"It was a natural mistake," I said. "It was exactly the same shape and size as a tea bag. It was even the same colour."

"A blatant case of misrepresentation, I'd say." Henrietta slipped the parcel into her anorak pocket. "Would you like to see the horses?" she enquired.

I could hardly refuse. Once we were outside I hoped that I would be able to make my escape. As it was I allowed myself to be conducted to the stables.

The stable block had once been grand. It was built in the traditional square with a clock arch. The stables were lovely, large, airy loose boxes with blue brick floors and green three-quarter tiled walls. There were cobblestones and a lead water trough, a dovecote and a proper mounting block. It was the sort of stable yard I had dreamed of working in, except that the same air of shabby neglect I had seen everywhere else was here as well, only more so. The paint on the woodwork had long flaked away, broken windows were stuffed with rags or patched with cardboard, doors hung at drunken angles, tiles were missing from the roofs and grass grew unchecked between the cobbles.

Henrietta led the way into a tack room where a jumble of saddlery was heaped up anyhow on a table. She untangled a brittle-looking headcollar and presented the damp little parcel to a large black and white cat who was curled up on a moth-eaten day rug. The cat sniffed it suspiciously and backed off. He jumped down from the table and stalked off with his tail in the air, looking offended. "Ungrateful beast," Henrietta said.

The first horse was a gaunt, ewe-necked thorough-bred mare who rolled her eyes and seemed disinclined to leave her stable. Henrietta flipped her in the ribs with the headcollar rope and she flew out of the door like a champagne cork and skidded on the cobbles.

"This is the old bay mare," Nigella said.

I stroked the old mare's faded brown face. The deep hollows above her eyes were full of dust.

"What's her name?" I asked.

Nigella looked blank. "She hasn't actually got a name," she said. "She's just the old bay mare."

The old bay mare scuttled back into her stable. There was a bit of a set-to with the black horse who lived next door. He dived round the box and refused to have anything to do with Henrietta who was finally obliged to grab him by the tail, whereupon he gave in and dropped his nose into the headcollar. Out in the yard he assumed an anxious expression and began to prance on the spot, lifting each of his legs in turn, as if he was performing a *piaffe*.

"He has a lot of nervous energy," Nigella explained. "He simply *never* stands still. It's very wearing and inconvenient at times, but he's perfectly all right when hounds are running, he goes like a bomb."

The black horse's stable had blocked drains and the bedding squelched. The soles of his prancing feet showed the soggy, smelly indications of thrush. I noticed these things and my heart sank into my boots.

Henrietta led the next horse out for inspection with the headcollar yanked up so tightly that I imagined that he must surely be throttled. But the grey horse didn't appear to notice. He was preoccupied with Higher Things. He put on a noble expression and stared into the distance above our heads as if we were beneath his notice.

"This is The Comet," Nigella said. "He's a bolter."

Bolter or not, The Comet presented a fine picture standing four square on the cobbles. Somehow it didn't seem to matter that his coat was streaked with yellow and the top of his tail resembled a scrubbing brush. "We've tried everything to improve his braking system," Nigella said. "Martingales, gag snaffles, twisted bits and check reins, but nothing makes the slightest difference. He just sets his neck and away he goes."

"Luckily he always heads for home," Henrietta said. "Which could be regarded as an advantage. Although it must be said that he has lost us some very good clients."

"I don't suppose he would be suitable for eventing?" Nigella suggested. "He is a very fast horse and he is as brave as a lion."

But even without looking at his mouth, I could see that The Comet was past it. "He is the right size," I said. "About sixteen-three, and he is the right type, threequarter-bred; but he is too old and besides, a horse with a good mouth and a controllable nature is a prime requirement for eventing. After all, it isn't a race. Think of the show-jumping. Think of the dressage." So as not to damn the horse completely, I said, "I suppose you have tried schooling?"

Henrietta looked astonished. "School The Comet?" she said incredulously. "What a joke." She dragged the grey horse back into the stable and removed the headcollar.

"We shall have to sell him, I suppose," Nigella said. "It seems a shame to part with such an impressive animal, but what else can we do?"

"We'll send him to auction," Henrietta decided. "Without a warranty. It's the only way to get rid of him. People who know him wouldn't have him as a gift."

I looked at a bad-tempered chestnut gelding who swished his tail, flattened his ears and made snapping noises with his teeth and I thought of the grey horse. I imagined him standing under the hammer, wearing his noble expression as the bids flew. Then I imagined him later, when his reputation had spread and he was known in every sale ring in the country as the grey horse who was a confirmed bolter. I could visualize his final destination only too well, and the fact that he would meet his fate with that same lofty indifference only made it harder to bear.

Henrietta now produced a moth-eaten roan with tall boxy feet like a donkey's. "This is Nelson," she said.

Nelson regarded us solemnly out of his one eye.

The eyelids of the other had been stitched together over the empty socket after some fearsome accident which didn't bear thinking about. I looked in despair at his scurfy coat and his hollow flanks, and the way in which, once back in his stable, he took a few wisps of dry hay in his soft little mouth and chewed them with every appearance of discomfort.

I knew I had to harden my heart to all this. I told myself firmly that sentiment didn't pay. I couldn't possibly come here, I couldn't take the job, it was out of the question. If I came to work in this awful place it would be the end, the absolute finish of my eventing ambitions. I would never find a sponsor to provide me with a decent horse. I would never get the chance I so desperately wanted. I would be sunk before I had even begun. The only thing to do was to leave at once. I would plead a pressing engagement. I would make my excuses now, straight away.

I turned to Nigella. "What exactly do you mean by pocket money wages?" I asked.

Nigella led the way past a row of stables which housed two hunter liveries. They were considered not worth looking at. She seemed embarrassed by this mention of hard cash, as if it was something one never mentioned in polite company.

"You would have to ask Mummy," she told me. "She isn't actually here at the moment. It's her Meals-on-Wheels day."

Henrietta brought out the last horse in the yard. It was a stunningly beautiful bay mare.

"Isn't she lovely," Nigella breathed. "I should be used to her by now, I know. But she still takes me by surprise every time I see her."

The bay mare stretched out her long elegant neck

and nuzzled Henrietta's pocket. Her coat was fine and smooth and her legs and her tail were silky black. Her eyes were dark and gentle and on her face there was a perfectly shaped star.

"She's terribly well bred," Nigella said. She recited an impressive pedigree.

"She was unbeaten in the show ring as a four-year-old," Henrietta said. "Champion at the Royal and practically every other County Show you can think of."

I said I could quite believe it.

"Of course," Nigella admitted. "That was before it happened."

"Before what happened?" I said faintly.

"Before she started to slip her stifle," Henrietta said.

I wasn't surprised; after all the other defective horses I had seen, if the bay mare had been fitted with an artificial limb, I would hardly have batted an eyelid.

"When that happened," Henrietta continued, "she was sold as a brood mare."

"She was still a very valuable animal," Nigella said. "Because of her breeding. She sold for well over four figures."

"Then what happened?" I said.

"Then they discovered that she was barren," Nigella said sadly.

"So we bought her," Henrietta said, slapping the mare heartily on her neck. "Because she was the most fantastic bargain, and she was the most beautiful horse we had ever seen."

"But that means you just keep her as a pet," I said, astonished. "If you can't breed with her and you can't ride her either!" I was amazed that people in such obviously straitened circumstances had given a home to a totally useless animal. By this act of mercy, Henrietta and Nigella soared in my estimation. I could almost overlook their shortcomings in stable management. They were redeemed.

"Can't ride her?" Henrietta said, frowning. "Of course we can ride her."

"If we couldn't breed with her and we couldn't ride her either, there would really be no point in keeping her," Nigella explained carefully. "Horses are very costly animals to keep. The price of corn alone is astronomical."

"Not to mention hay and shoeing," Henrietta added. "And you can't even get free straw in return for stable manure any longer, not like the old days."

"But what about the slipped stifle," I wondered. "Is it cured?"

"Oh no," Nigella said. "It still happens. When it does, we just turn her away for a month or however long it takes to come right again."

"But you don't hire her out for hunting," I said. "Not when you know it could happen at any moment."

"It doesn't happen every day," Henrietta pointed out. "To be fair, she sometimes lasts half a season. And nobody has ever complained." She grinned.

"They are always too worried about the mare," Nigella said, suppressing a giggle. "They think they have broken her leg. They are terrified almost out of their wits."

"They think they are going to be sued," Henrietta spluttered. "They think we will make them pay for the horse!"

I had to laugh. It was grotesque. It was just too awful for words. We all leaned on the bay mare and the tears poured down our cheeks. I forgot all about my sponsor and my future prospects and when Nigella suggested that I should start work next week, I was too shattered to argue.

2

Mutual Disagreements

When I rang Lady Jennifer to get some hard facts about the job she was enthusiastic but evasive. "But my *dear*," she cried in ringing tones when I enquired about hours of work and days off. "You will be such an *enormous* help to us all, a marvellous asset! We shall be most *understanding* about your days off. It will be such *fun* to have another young person about the place, we have no other help whatsoever – you can't *imagine* the turmoil we live in!"

Actually, I could imagine it only too well. As soon as I could get a word in edgeways, I enquired about the pocket money wages.

"But of course you shall have pocket money," Lady Jennifer trilled. "We wouldn't *dream* of expecting you to help out without remuneration! We shall come to a mutual agreement the very *second* you arrive. You are intending to arrive?" she added with a trace of anxiety. "You haven't changed your mind?"

I said I hadn't. It hardly seemed the moment to mention that I was only accepting the job on a temporary basis, until something more promising turned up.

"And what about your parents?" Lady Jennifer wanted to know. "Do you think I should have a *teeny* little word? Just to reassure them that their daughter will be in excellent hands? To say how absolutely *thrilled* we are? After all, you are only seventeen . . ."

"I don't think so," I said hastily. "I really don't see the necessity."

My father heartily disapproved of my desire to work with horses and the fifteen interviews had left him feeling distinctly edgy, especially in view of the fact that many of my school friends were already propping up the dole queue. He had seen my six month apprenticeship at a top training establishment as a complete waste of time and energy, despite the fact that I had been accepted on a Working Pupil basis and had paid for my instruction myself with hours of hard labour every day. I had gained a qualification at the end of it, but still he wasted no opportunity to remind me that in his opinion, the horse world had nothing to offer but low pay, bleak prospects, and broken promises.

It went against the grain to admit to myself that he might be right. Certainly there seemed to be no jobs vacant in eventing yards at all, and the two jobs I had been offered as a result of the fourteen interviews had both been in dubious little riding schools offering squalid accommodation in caravans and a few pounds in return for a 70 hour week. With the Fanes at least I would be able to hunt, and as the hunting field was supposed to be the best training ground for event horses and riders, I wouldn't be completely wasting my time. Also, it was a relief to be able to tell my father that I had landed a job at last, but as I knew he would take a dim view of the pocket money wages, I decided that the less he knew about the job the better.

It was agreed that I should arrive by train the

following Monday. Lady Jennifer met me at the station and I could hear her voice even before I got off the train. She was a tall, thin person in a crumpled raincoat and a headscarf the size of a small tablecloth. Like the black horse, she seemed to have a lot of nervous energy and she threw the tiny station into confusion by blocking the passenger exit with her delapidated shooting brake.

"I won't keep you waiting a *minute* longer than necessary," she shrilled at the trapped passengers. "It's so *frightfully* thoughtless of me, I can't think *why* I did it. I must have been *insane* to park here." She emptied her handbag on to the bonnet in a fruitless effort to find the car keys and finally located them in the ignition.

Whilst all this was going on I was loading my case into the back. I had wondered why all the windows were steamed up and when I opened the rear doors I could see why; the shooting brake was full of hounds. They were sitting on all the seats and I couldn't imagine where I was going to sit. I considered the passenger seat. The two lemon and white hounds who occupied it regarded me in an encouraging manner. The nearest one had a long dribble of saliva suspended from its dewlap. I decided on the back seat. The four hounds already seated shuffled up obligingly to make room and arranged their heads four deep in order to inspect my person.

Lady Jennifer got into the driving seat and slammed the door. This acted like a starter's pistol to the hounds, who dived into position for the journey. The two on the passenger seat put their front paws on the dashboard and pressed their noses to the windscreen. My neighbours put their paws on the back of the front seats and craned forward avidly as the shooting brake bucketed away. The smell of dog was overpowering.

"You won't mind if we drop the young entry off first?" Lady Jennifer enquired, swerving to avoid a cyclist and causing a hound to slip off the dashboard and hit its chin on the glove compartment. "We walked them this summer and they *will* keep coming back. I can't *tell* you how inconvenient it is. The Hunt Staff get *furious*."

I hoped the young entry didn't live very far away. If they did I thought I should possibly suffocate before we got there. I wound down the window in an effort to get some fresh air. As soon as they got wind of this, all four hounds launched themselves across me and jammed their heads out as far as their shoulders, pinning me back in the seat. I managed to extract myself from the jungle of hind legs and waving sterns and gained the comparative comfort of the empty end of the seat. I didn't dare open the window.

Lady Jennifer applied the brakes smartly outside a collection of whitewashed buildings. A sign announced that we had arrived at the Midvale and Westbury Hunt Kennels. This was a relief, but as soon as the shooting brake juddered to a stop our hounds dived under the seats as one man. They refused to budge. Lady Jennifer and I were obliged to drag them out by the scruff of their necks whilst they pretended to be dead. Once out of the brake they crept across the yard with their sterns dragging on the concrete. They looked anything but happy to be home.

Lady Jennifer unbolted the iron grille door of the

exercise yard with furtive care and we stuffed our hounds inside. In a trice they had cheered up and were indistinguishable from the rest of the pack. We might have got away undetected but they put their paws up on the bars with the rest and set up a terrific racket. The noise brought a young man in a white kennel coat to the door of one of the buildings. He looked rather cross.

Lady Jennifer decided that attack was the best form of defence. "William," she shrilled indignantly. "Your hounds have been trespassing *again*. They have upset all my refuse bins. I simply will *not* tolerate it. If it happens again I shall have them shot."

William looked taken aback by this. He went rather red. He opened his mouth to say something, but Lady Jennifer was already on a different tack.

"Elaine," she said briskly. "This is William, the Second Whipper-in. William, this is Elaine, our new groom." She made for the shooting brake. It was all very awkward.

"Hello," I said. "I'm sorry about the hounds. I'm sure she wouldn't really have them shot."

William didn't reply. He just stared. He ran his hand through his ginger hair and left it standing in peaks, stiff with bran. "New *groom*," he said in disbelief. "New *groom?*"

"That's right," I said. "New groom."

William still didn't know what to make of it. He turned and shouted to someone inside the building. "Hey, Forster! Come out here a minute! The Galloping Fanes have gone and got themselves a groom!"

I wasn't sure that I liked the sound of this. I

looked round for the shooting brake but Lady Jennifer was having trouble of her own with the gears. Terrible crashing and grinding noises accompanied the shunting backwards and forwards.

Forster had the kind of looks that belong to dangerous young men in novels. He had a dark handsome face and black hair that curled almost to the collar of his coat. I could tell he thought himself rather special by the way he leaned indolently against the door frame and looked me up and down in an amused sort of way.

"You must be barmy," he drawled, "to go and work with that collection of old screws."

For one terrible moment I thought he meant Lady Jennifer and her daughters. Then I realized that he was referring to the horses.

"You have seen the place?" William wanted to know. "You do know what it's like? You have *seen* the horses?"

"Horses!" Forster gave a contemptuous laugh. "There isn't a sound animal in the yard, or a properly fed one either. The Fanes don't need a groom, they need a knacker."

"As long as they don't call us," William said, grinning. "We don't want them. All the hirelings boiled up together wouldn't feed hounds for more than a week."

I didn't want to listen to any more of this.

"Excuse me," I said. "I have to go."

"Wait a minute," William said. "I asked you if you had seen the place. You wouldn't be going there sight unseen would you? You haven't taken the job *blind*?"

24

There was genuine concern in his voice but I was so offended by their attitude that I hardly noticed.

"Yes, I've seen the place," I said crossly. "And I've seen the horses, so I know what it's like. But it might interest you to know that things are going to be rather different in future. We are going to reorganize the yard and the business. There are going to be a lot of improvements." I looked round anxiously for the shooting brake and saw that it was moving in my direction.

"And who is going to pay for these improvements?" Forster enquired in a sceptical tone.

"More to the point," William added, "who's going to pay you?"

"That's my affair," I snapped. As the shooting brake came alongside with the passenger door flapping, I jumped in and slammed the door as hard as I could. The crash caused Lady Jennifer's foot to slip off the clutch. As we bounced away Forster was laughing his silly head off. The last impression I got of him was that his teeth were sickeningly white.

If Lady Jennifer was alarmed by this show of temper in her new employee, she didn't show it. She hummed a little tune as she drove in her erratic manner along the Suffolk lanes heaped with golden leaves. I was too preoccupied to notice the glory of it. I sat in silence and I wondered, not for the first time, what I had let myself in for. I realized that the callous comments which had made me so angry, were probably no more than the truth. But if I had been a fool to accept responsibility for a bunch of old crocks, if I had been a worse fool to accept a job with no prospects and quite possibly no money either, I didn't want to be told so, not yet, and certainly not by Forster or William. I had to give it a try first. I had to give it a chance.

As the shooting brake flew along the lanes, leaving eddies of leaves in its wake, I grew more optimistic. It would give me great satisfaction, I decided, to show the Midvale and Westbury Hunt a thing or two. In my imagination I saw the Fanes' tumble-down yard restored to its former grandeur. It could be the finest livery stable in the county. We could have the most luxurious loose boxes, the most magnificent stable yard, the cleanest tack and the fittest, best turned-out horses that ever graced the hunting field. Not only that, but we could have the best hirelings available anywhere. My imagination soared. By my own skill I saw myself turning my collection of lame ducks into beautiful equine swans, so expertly produced, so superbly schooled, that people would queue up to ride them.

Untrimmed branches pinging against the sides of the shooting brake brought me back to earth. We turned in at the lodge gates where one vulpine creature leered down from the top of its post and the other lay nose down in the grass, choked with ivy.

"Welcome to Havers Hall," Lady Jennifer said. She leaned over unexpectedly and squeezed my hand with her long, bony fingers as the shooting brake bucked and leapt over the pot-holes.

Nigella and Henrietta were waiting, a reception committee of two on the front steps. If anything, they looked even scruffier than I remembered them. They grabbed my cases and bore me up into the hall as Lady Jennifer swerved off round the back of the house in a shower of gravel.

"Welcome to our humble home," Nigella said brightly. "Family seat of the Fanes for eight generations."

"Clobbered by death duties, turned down by the National Trust," Henrietta added. "And shortly to be condemned by the local council."

I wasn't sure if this was supposed to be a joke or not. I smiled politely. The hall was vast and icy cold. There were no carpets and precious little in the way of furniture either. The ornate plaster ceiling was patched with damp and mould. The two huge stone fireplaces which dominated either end were heaped with dead ash.

"It isn't very cosy, is it?" Henrietta said. "I expect it's a bit stark for your taste?"

"It's certainly very large," I said. "And very grand."

"*Was* very grand, you mean," Henrietta said peevishly. "You may as well say what you think."

"Take no notice of Henrietta," Nigella said. "She gets a bit prickly at times. She can't help it. She finds it hard to accept that she is one of the *nouveaux pauvres*."

"I'm not poor," Henrietta objected. "Can anyone be described as poor," she asked me, "who owns a Vile secretaire?" She led the way up the dusty wide staircase. Her wellingtons squeaked on the bare oak treads.

I wasn't sure what a secretaire was. "I wonder you keep it," I said. "If it's so awful."

Henrietta paused to look at me in astonishment. "It isn't awful," she said. "It's magnificent."

"Vile is the name of the maker," Nigella

27

explained. "William Vile. Henrietta's very proud of her secretaire, it's her dowry."

We walked along a gallery landing lined with darkened oil paintings. Now and again there was a gap and a rectangular patch of lighter coloured wall.

"Do people have dowries these days?" I asked.

"I don't think so," Nigella said. "It's a pretty feudal idea. Still, Henrietta has hers."

Henrietta opened one of the doors along the landing and I followed them into a large, dark room filled with an unwholesome smell of damp. There was a chill air in the room which brought out goose-flesh at the back of my neck. In the half light I could make out a vast, carved wardrobe, a bed of unusual height and solidity, and another huge, empty stone fireplace. The only other furniture was a dark oak chest, shaped like a coffin. Henrietta began to heave mightily at some wooden shutters which stretched from floor to ceiling.

"Well?" Nigella said in an uncertain tone. "What do you think?" She dumped my case on the single piece of threadbare carpet. "Do you like it?"

I didn't like it. I didn't like the dark, or the cold, or the smell. As my eyes got used to the gloom I saw other things that I didn't like. There was a dead jackdaw in the hearth. There was an angry Eliza-bethan lady on the wall. She clutched an orb to her chest and she glared at me balefully, as if the whole of her misfortune must surely be my fault. It was terrible. It was frightening. I had never been in such an alarming room in all of my life. I tried to work out how I was going to tell Nigella that I couldn't sleep here. Not possibly. I wouldn't dare to close my eyes even for a minute. I tried to find the right words to explain how I felt without causing offence. And all the time Henrietta yanked at the shutters and Nigella waited expectantly for me to speak.

I took a deep breath and suddenly Henrietta and the shutters flew aside with a resounding crash. October sunshine flooded over us and the room was filled with the warm, earthy smell of grass and dying leaves and plough. Across the park I saw old turf like worn velvet, and oak trees, red and golden. The river lay like a blue and silver ribbon and all along the banks the willows leaned. Beyond, the Suffolk landscape stretched, brown and green and gilded and somewhere, even beyond that, was the sea.

"Oh," I said. "It's perfect. It's absolutely beautiful."

"I'm so glad," Nigella said with relief. "It wouldn't be everyone's idea of a comfortable room."

After a conducted tour of the mahogany panelled bathroom and a recital of its deficiencies, Nigella left me to unpack. Henrietta didn't follow straight away. She stood thoughtfully in the doorway and watched me stow my belongings in the giant wardrobe. She had picked up the dead jackdaw and she swung it by the legs in an absent-minded manner, as if it was a handbag.

"You must have been pretty desperate for a job to come here," she said unexpectedly. "I don't expect you will stay."

"Not stay?" I said. "Why shouldn't I stay?"

"Because you want to event. Because you only took the job until you can find something more suitable. Because this is an awful place," Henrietta said. "And you know it."

29

"It isn't true," I said. "It's a very nice place. Of course I shall stay."

I couldn't look at her. I kept my eyes on my new breeches, my eventing breeches, strapped with soft creamy suede, and still in their tissue wraps. Unworn. When I looked up, Henrietta had gone.

I covered up the Elizabethan lady with my tweed jacket. She didn't seem quite so angry any more, but I couldn't stand the accusation in her eyes.

3

A Nice Long List

Supper was served at the kitchen table. Nigella grabbed roaring hot plates out of the Aga which, she explained, was having one of its over-enthusiastic days. The plates warmed our faces and stuck to the table. They were crusted with dried up mince decorated with solidified potato and peas like lead shot. It was probably left over from the Meals-on-Wheels.

Lady Jennifer was not present at this repast, having departed for some committee meeting or other clad in a suit which dated from the New Look and a Hermes scarf with a small darn in it. When Nigella had distributed some frighteningly strong, bitter coffee and woody apples, I suggested that she might like to outline the daily stable routine for my benefit.

"Stable routine?" Nigella said, and her eyebrows rose up and vanished into her thatch of a fringe.

"We don't actually have a routine," Henrietta said absently. She dangled her apple peel which she had carefully cut into a long curly spiral from her little finger. "Do I throw it over my left shoulder or my right?" she wondered.

"You must have some sort of routine," I said. "You must do certain jobs at certain times."

"Isn't she thinking of salt?" Nigella wanted to know. "Isn't it salt you throw over your shoulder?"

I said I thought it was. "What time do you start in the mornings?" I asked her. "What do you do first?"

"We feed first," Nigella said. "Doesn't everyone feed first?"

"I think apple peel probably only works on Halloween night," Henrietta said glumly. She threw the spiral over her shoulder anyway. It landed in the sink.

"Then what do you do?" I said.

"Then we muck out," Nigella said.

Henrietta went over to the sink and peered into the clutter of dirty dishes. "It's a W," she decided.

"W for William," Nigella said.

"William," Henrietta said in disgust. "Who on earth would want *William*." She came back to the table and began to hack savagely at her naked apple.

"When do you do the watering?" I persisted. "When do you give the horses their hay?"

"Look," Henrietta said in an irritated tone. "You're not at the training centre now. You can forget all about routines and things. We don't have them."

I could see that I was going to have to make a firm stand if anything at all was to be achieved. "If we are going to reorganize the yard," I said, "we shall have to work to a routine. It's the only way to be efficient."

"And if there is one thing we need to be," Nigella said in a heartfelt voice, "it's efficient."

"I thought I might spend my first day mucking out," I suggested. I knew that the loose boxes hadn't been cleaned out properly for months, possibly years, and that the corners were packed solid.

"It won't take you all day," Henrietta said. "Even if you do the lot."

"It might," I said, "if I do each one properly. If I turn out all the bedding and disinfect the floors and flush out the drains. If I wash down the tiles and scrub out the mangers and the water buckets."

"That *will* be lovely," Nigella said.

I knew it wouldn't be.

"If I look after the stable work," I said, "you will both be free to cope with the exercising."

There was a silence.

"We don't exercise the horses every day," Nigella said cautiously. "We couldn't possibly. We only take them out on alternate days, if that. On the days they are not ridden, we turn them out for a few hours in the park."

"But hunters need to be taken out every day," I said. "They should have been having steady road work every day for months already to strengthen their limbs and to build muscle, to condition their hearts and their lungs. If they are not exercised properly, how do you expect them to get fit?" I had been on a tour of inspection before supper and I knew that none of the horses was even half fit. It occurred to me that perhaps they didn't need to be. That half a day's hunting on one of the Fanes' hirelings would be enough for anybody.

"I don't know how you expect us to exercise nine horses every day *and* do all the stable work," Henrietta said crossly, "when we haven't any staff. When you know perfectly well that we've been without any help whatsoever."

"We've done our best," Nigella added. "But no two people could cope with nine stabled horses. It

33

just isn't possible." She stared down at her apple pips and assumed an air of total exhaustion.

All this was hardly encouraging, but on my tour of inspection I had discovered several deficiencies that I felt bound to mention. I decided to get it over with.

"The tack room will have to be sorted out," I said. "It's a disgrace. Some of the tack will have to be replaced. We need pegs and saddle brackets. We need Neat's Foot oil and metal polish. We need thread for repairs and needles and soap. And that's not all. There are other things."

"Oh?" Henrietta said in an uneasy voice. "What other things?"

"There only seems to be one set of grooming tools," I said. "We need more. The horses need to be clipped. We need clippers and blankets, rugs and rollers and bandages."

Nigella was looking alarmed.

"Is that all?" Henrietta enquired. "I wonder you can't think of anything else. Perhaps we can find you a pencil and some paper. Then you can make a nice long list."

"What a very good idea," I said.

There was another silence whilst I waited for the pencil and paper. Nobody moved.

"We never make lists," Nigella said awkwardly.

"I shall need the vet," I continued. "To rasp Nelson's back teeth. He has some nasty sharp edges very high up and he can't chew his food properly. I shall need the blacksmith as well. There is hardly a horse in the yard whose feet don't need attention and anyway, I need him to pare away some of the

34

black horse's foot, so that I can treat the thrushy bits."

"Hrmm," Henrietta said.

"What exactly do you mean by 'hrmm'?" I said impatiently.

"Heavens," Nigella said hastily. "Did you say thrush?"

"Also," I said, warming to my theme. "There isn't much in the feed room."

"There almost never is," Nigella admitted.

"There's hardly any bran left. The corn bin is only a quarter full."

"I don't know why you are telling us all this," Henrietta grumbled. "It isn't as if we don't already know."

"The horses need to put in condition," I said. "They are far too poor to start the season. As they are, they won't last a month. We need high protein food. We need fatteners. Some of the horses need boiled food, especially the old." I stopped myself just in time from adding "the lame and the sick".

"You are absolutely right," Nigella said. "We do." She stared unhappily into her coffee. It had gone cold and it was covered with a fragile metallic skin.

"We need barley and linseed. We need chaff for mixing, and sugar beet pulp. We need high energy foods, oats and barley and cubes. There isn't any rock salt."

"All these things we suddenly need," Henrietta said in an acid tone. "We never needed them before."

"You need them now," I said.

"Only because you say so," Henrietta snapped.

I tried not to lose my temper, but it was hard to

understand their attitude. They seemed totally unwilling to grasp the realities of the situation.

"Look," I said. "Either you want to run a decent yard, or you don't."

"Oh, we do," Nigella assured me. "We really do."

"What you don't seem to realize," Henrietta said, "is how incredibly difficult it is to manage. How impossibly expensive things are. Look at hay, for instance."

"I did," I said. "There's only half a ton in the barn."

"Is that all?" Nigella said. "I didn't realize we were as low as that. It won't last any time at all."

"It certainly won't," I said. "Especially if we feed by the book and allow the horses all the hay they can eat."

"As you seem to do everything by the book," Henrietta said waspishly. "Maybe you should consult it on our behalf. It might tell us how we are going to pay for all these things you expect us to provide at the drop of a hat. Or perhaps you intend to pay for them out of your own pocket?"

"I can't pay for them," I said. "I'm absolutely broke. I've been out of work for four months and I'm down to my last pound."

"Then you know how *we* feel," Henrietta said, "because we haven't a bean either."

"Not to put too fine a point on it," Nigella said despondently, "we're at a very low ebb. Financially, I mean."

They both looked depressed.

There was a lengthy silence whilst we all thought about it. Henrietta filled in the time by picking little

bits of crinkly wood from the sleeve of her jumper.
Then she piled the bits into a pyramid on her plate.

"Of course," I said eventually. "Increased efficiency doesn't necessarily have to cost money."

"A few minutes ago," Henrietta pointed out, "it sounded very expensive."

"After all," I said, trying to be optimistic, "the hunting season is only a couple of weeks away."

"Is it really?" Nigella said. "As soon as that?"

"And that means," I went on, "that there will be money coming in from the hirelings."

"Which, according to you," Henrietta reminded me, "won't last a month."

"And then there are the liveries," I continued.

"When they pay," Nigella said. "Which doesn't seem to be too often."

"I shall make sure that they pay," I said firmly, "and as we improve the yard, we shall get more."

"Get more liveries?" Nigella said, interested. "How will we get more?"

"By recommendation," I said. "We could even advertise."

"We're not very good at advertisements," Henrietta commented.

"There are plenty of spare boxes," I said. "There's no shortage of room. We are in the ideal position, the Hunt is almost on the doorstep. Even one really high class livery would add tone to the yard."

"Tone," Nigella said warmly, "is just what we need."

"The boxes are beautifully built," I said. "The yard is rather splendid." I pushed away the memory of the missing tiles, the broken windows and the peeling paint. Even the empty corn bins receded.

"The hacking must be marvellous, especially now, when there are miles and miles of stubble fields; and where else could livery clients ride in such a beautiful park?"

"It's true," Nigella agreed. "Our facilities are ideal. We are in the perfect situation. I can't imagine *why* we get so depressed."

"We'll give it a try," Henrietta decided. "You can have a free hand. We will do it your way, even though it entails lists and graphs and charts. Whenever it is possible, we will do it by the book."

"And in the morning, Henrietta and I will exercise every horse," Nigella promised. "We will make a fresh start. We simply can't *help* but be successful."

It seemed to me that we couldn't afford not to be.

4

If Something Isn't Done . . .

True to their word, the next morning Nigella and Henrietta prepared to give their attention to the exercising.

"How many hours of exercise does each horse have to be given on this daily routine of yours?" Henrietta enquired, peering over the half door into the black horse's stable.

"Two," I said. I was scrubbing out the black horse's feet with soap and water and he wasn't enjoying it one little bit. Finding his legs immobilized, he was obliged to content himself with rolling his eyes, snaking his neck, and rotating his tail like a windmill.

Nigella's head appeared beside Henrietta's. "Two hours?" she exclaimed. "You do realize that means eighteen hours of exercising *every* day? Nine hours solid riding for each of us. You can't be *serious*."

"Of course I'm serious," I said. "You can double up. You can take two horses each." I let go of the black horse's foot and he pumped his leg up and down a few times in an anxious sort of way, to reassure himself that it still worked. I had scrubbed out the evil-smelling gunge in the cleft of his frogs and trimmed the ragged bits. He didn't seem to be lame and I thought that if I could treat the rotten bits with Stockholm tar and keep him on a dry bed, he probably wouldn't need professional treatment.

He did need the blacksmith though, his shoes were paper thin.

"I don't see why we shouldn't," Nigella said. "One of the liveries has lost a shoe, so he can't do any road work; that leaves eight horses to exercise, so if we take four out at a time . . ."

"Four at a time," Henrietta said in alarm. "Four!"

"Not each," Nigella said patiently. "Two each. Four altogether. One lot in the mornings and one in the afternoons."

"Better still," I said, "one lot before breakfast, and one lot after. Then we shall have more time."

"More time for what?" Henrietta said.

"More time for strapping, tack cleaning, renovating, painting and weeding," I said. I stepped out of the way of the black horse who was having an experimental trot round the box, lifting his scrubbed feet like a hackney.

"Sometimes," Henrietta said in her clear voice as they departed in the direction of the tack room, "it's better not to ask."

For the first period of exercise, Nigella decided to ride the old bay mare and lead the black horse, and Henrietta elected to ride the bad-tempered chestnut and lead The Comet. There was a bit of a fracas when the old bay mare decided she didn't like the idea of communal exercise and refused to leave the yard. She suddenly dug in her toes and jibbed so strongly that Nigella was forced to let go of the black horse. He decided that his stable was the safest place and dived off past the bad-tempered chestnut who, not being one to let a golden opportunity pass by, lunged forward with bared teeth and almost displaced Henrietta, who was fiddling with her stirrup leathers. The Comet, unimpressed by all these goings-on, stood rocklike on the cobbles, even though his withered leading rein had snapped and dangled uselessly under his chin. Eventually, the black horse was captured, an even more withered rein was clipped on to The Comet, and they clattered off leaving me to do battle with the black horse's drains.

It took me ages to clear all the sour, soggy straw out of the stable and to scrape out the sides and the corners. I trundled six wheel-barrow loads to the steaming, sprawling muck heap behind the barn. Then I swept out the stable and prised off the drain cover. I poked about hopefully for a while with the end of the pitchfork, but it was packed solid. In the end there seemed nothing for it but to unblock it by hand. I steeled myself to the task and laid a sack down on the bricks. I was lying on my stomach with my arm down the drain up to my armpit, groping in the unspeakable depths, when I heard footsteps. Footsteps and voices.

"I've just about had a beakful of this place," an angry female voice proclaimed. "I can't stand the lousy dump a minute longer. What's more," the voice went on, getting angrier by the second, "I'm going to find the Misses Fane and tell them so, just you see if I . . ."

The voice tailed off as the footsteps came to an abrupt halt outside the stable. A large person wearing pink dungarees stretched to the very limits of their endurance appeared in the doorway. She had cropped hair dyed a stark white blonde, and her red, rather puffy face was decorated with a cupid bow of

41

chalky pink lipstick, hooped eyebrows, and a matching pothook at the corner of each eye drawn with thick orange pencil.

"Who the devil are you?" she demanded in a belligerent tone.

A dead white face framed by a floppy pageboy haircut peered round the dungarees. When the face spotted me lying on the sack it gave a little yelp.

"I'm Elaine," I managed to say. "I work here." I couldn't get up at once because I had finally managed to get my fingers round the last solid plug of filth. It came away suddenly, with a loud sucking plop and a shower of evil-smelling black droplets. The Pink Dungarees didn't flinch, but the white face ducked.

"*Work* here?" the Pink Dungarees exclaimed in tones of disbelief. "Since *when*?"

The owner of the white face came out from behind the dungarees in order to gape at me in stupefaction. She was a small, thin girl of about fourteen. I scrambled to my feet. I was splattered all over with liquid manure and I knew that I reeked.

"Since this morning," I said. "I've only just started, so I haven't had time to get anything organized yet." I wiped the worst of the black stuff off on to the sack in case anyone offered to shake hands. They didn't.

"And who the hell are you to organize anything?" Pink Dungarees said scornfully, planting her hands on her hips.

"I'm qualified," I said. "I've got my Horsemasters Certificate."

"You and a thousand others," Pink Dungarees

scoffed. "Who do you think you're going to impress with that?"

"I trained with Hans Gelderhol," I said.

A glimmer of interest appeared between the pothooks. "Gelderhol the Eventer?"

"Is there another Gelderhol?" I enquired.

"*Gelderhol*," the white-faced girl said in a breathless voice. "You trained with Gelderhol?"

"Shut it, Doreen," Pink Dungarees snapped. She was determined not to be impressed.

"All the same," Doreen breathed. "*Gelderhol*."

"Gelderhol or not," Pink Dungarees said. "It'll take more than you to lick this hole into shape. It'll take an army."

"I may get one," I said. "I may take working pupils." I had only just thought of it. It seemed a splendid idea.

"Trainees," Pink Dungarees said in disgust. "They're *all* we need. Anyhow, who'd want to train in a dump like this?"

"It won't be a dump when I've finished with it," I said in an annoyed tone. I wasn't prepared to spend the morning sparring with Pink Dungarees. I had far too much to do.

"You're not being very fair, Brenda," the white-faced girl said, suddenly showing a bit of spirit. "You're not really giving her much of a chance."

"She hasn't got much of a chance," Pink Dungarees retorted. "Not working for the Fanes; where the devil are they anyway?" She glared round the yard as if she expected to catch them hiding somewhere.

"The Fanes are out exercising," I said crossly. "They won't be back for at least an hour. So I

43

suggest that you either tell me what you want, or go and wait somewhere for them to come back." I turned back into the stable, picked up the metal grid and jammed it back over the drain. I had wasted enough time. I picked up the stiff brush and began to sweep the drain clots towards the door.

"Now look here, Miss Busy Bee," Brenda said angrily. "I'll tell you what I want! What I want is a bit of service! A bit of value for money, that's what I want!"

I stopped sweeping. "Value for what money?" I said.

"You're not explaining yourself very well, Bren," the white-faced girl said anxiously. "She doesn't know who we are."

"*We*," Brenda pronounced, pursing her rosebud lips, "are livery clients. And what is more, *we* are not satisfied, and *if something is not done* about it, *we* are leaving."

"Oh, I wouldn't do that," I said hastily. I put the brush down. It hadn't occurred to me that I might be dealing with livery clients. The livery clients I had encountered at the training centre hadn't looked anything like Doreen and Brenda. They had been sober, middle-class sort of people who came into the yard dressed in tweed jackets and breeches and sometimes slipped the students fifty pence for saddling their horses. I cursed myself for being so offhand. After promising the Fanes more livery clients, the last thing I wanted on my first morning was to have to tell them they had two less. "I'm sorry," I said. "I didn't realize. If you tell me what's wrong, I'll do my best to put it right."

"You can get the bloody blacksmith to my horse,

44

for a start," Brenda said. "The creature's had a shoe off for a week and he's footsore. How can I get the beast fit without a decent set of shoes?"

"I'll organize it," I said. "Leave it to me. If I can, I'll get him here tomorrow."

"And where's the mineral supplement?" she said. "Ordered and paid for three weeks ago and still not arrived."

"I don't know," I admitted. "But I'll find out."

"My pony is supposed to have damped hay," Doreen said in her timid voice. "He's got a cough. He's supposed to have paste spread on his tongue twice a day. I don't think they remember."

"I'll remember," I promised. "I'll give him the paste. I'll dunk his hay."

"We'll give it one more week, Busy Bee," Doreen said threateningly. "If things don't look up, we're off."

"I quite understand," I said.

There was a lot of snorting and muttering and slamming of stable doors after this, but eventually the Pink Dungarees left, with Doreen scuttling along behind.

The next interruption wasn't long coming. I had just poured a bucket of water down the drain and was listening to the satisfying gurgle as it cleared, when there was a scraping noise at the door and two delighted faces appeared in the crack. The two faces were swiftly joined by four more. It was the young entry.

I was not at all pleased to see them. Apart from already having suffered one set-back in the form of Big Brenda, I knew that there was no way I could get the hounds back to the kennels as Lady Jennifer

45

had taken off earlier in the shooting brake, it being her day of duty at the Oxfam Shop. I rattled the bucket at them, hoping to frighten them away.

"Home," I commanded them sternly. "GO HOME."

But the young entry were overjoyed to hear my voice. They tried to fight their way in through the partly opened door and succeeded in trapping their shoulders and their necks to the accompaniment of howls, yelpings and choking noises. When I kicked at the door to free them, they burst into the stable and leapt at me in an ecstasy of lickings and slobberings. Their coats were wet and black and sticky where they had been rolling in the fields of burned stubble.

I was trying to stay on my feet, fending them off with the bucket, when I heard galloping hooves on the drive. I dropped the bucket and rushed outside with the young entry bounding at my heels, expecting to see an escapee. The Comet perhaps, or the old bay mare. It was Forster.

He was in his scarlet, mounted on a rangy liver chestnut whose coat was running with sweat. His boots were splattered with mud and his white breeches were streaked with black. He was in a blazing temper.

"Damn you, Ladybird, you useless cur," he raged as soon as he set eyes on the young entry. "And you, Landlord! Hike back there you bloody little fiends, or I'll break your miserable necks for you!"

He kicked his horse towards them, cracking his whip. The young entry cringed away and dived behind me for protection. I backed away from the plunging hooves, treading on paws and sterns as I went, setting up a succession of agonized yelpings.

"Don't you dare hit them," I shouted. "If you touch them with that whip, I'll report you to the RSPCA for cruelty!"

Forster gave a bark of laughter. I stood my ground, feeling foolish because of the young entry peering anxiously round and through my legs. "If they were well treated at the kennels," I said defensively, "they wouldn't keep coming back here."

Forster yanked the liver chestnut to a standstill. "They keep coming back," he said angrily, "because they were ruined by your crazy employers. They slept on the beds and gobbled scraps in the kitchen like lap dogs. These are supposed to be working hounds, not *curs*!" He threw a booted leg over the horse's neck and jumped down on to the cobbles. The liver chestnut dropped its head thankfully and let out a long, gusting sigh from its distended nostrils. "How would you feel," Forster said, "if you had been up since four, had a hard morning's cubbing, and then had to do a six mile detour because half the pack decided to go visiting?"

"I suppose I might feel a bit peeved," I said, keeping my eyes on the plaited leather thong with its muddy red lash flickering on the end like a serpent's tongue.

"Peeved," Forster said in disgust, "is not the word I would use to describe it." He coiled up his whip, and as if by magic the young entry crept out from behind my legs and prostrated themselves at his feet, grovelling and fawning in the most sycophantic manner possible. One of them actually started to lick his boots.

I was exasperated by this fickle behaviour and I

47

was also uncomfortably aware that I was still splattered with dried sludge from the black horse's stable. Normally, it wouldn't have mattered, but for some reason it mattered now.

"I suggest you take your toadying curs off back to the kennels," I said crossly. "You're not the only one with a job to do." I started to walk off, but Forster got hold of my elbow.

"Hold on a minute," he said. "I'm sorry if I frightened you. I was angry."

"Obviously," I said.

"They don't hate me, you know," he said, gesturing at the young entry, sprawling contentedly at his feet. "They have to learn discipline. If they don't, they can't hunt, and if they can't hunt, they have to be destroyed. It's as simple as that."

"It isn't simple," I said. "It's heartless."

"They're not pets," he said. "You couldn't keep a foxhound as a pet. They're hunters and scavengers by nature. They're not a domestic strain." One of the young entry laid its head on his knee and gazed up at him with adoration in its eyes. "So how's the job?" he asked.

"The job's OK," I said. "If you're really interested."

"If I wasn't interested," he said, "I wouldn't have asked."

"So now you've asked," I said, "and I've told you. So perhaps you'll let go of my arm."

"I'll consider it," he said.

We stood and stared at each other. I told myself that he was arrogant and conceited and heartless, and that I hated him. But he was in his scarlet, with his hounds at his feet. He was muddy and tired, and there was blood on his face where a bramble had jagged him. And the mocking, sneering façade was gone. So my eyes dropped first, and I felt the colour rush to my cheeks. I knew how very, very easy it would be to fall for Forster.

"Elaine," he said, letting go of my arm. "Why are you so determined to make a fool of yourself?"

"I don't know what you mean," I said faintly.

"The Fanes are the laughing stock of the county," he said. "Surely you realize that."

"I needed a job," I said.

"You don't need this job," he said. "I can get you a better one."

"Another job?" I looked up in surprise.

"Felix Hissey needs a groom. His girl's leaving. She's got," he hesitated, " . . . personal problems."

"Felix Hissey?" I said. "You mean Felix Hissey, the Pickle King?" I had heard of Felix Hissey. His company sponsored the two largest Three Day Events in the country. Not only that, but they awarded two annual scholarships so that promising young event riders and their horses could train with the National Coach. A job with someone like Felix Hissey was the golden opportunity I had been waiting for. I couldn't quite believe my ears. I wondered if it was Forster's idea of a joke. But he looked perfectly serious.

"He's a good employer," he said, mistaking my silence for lack of enthusiasm. "It's a well paid job. There's also a very nice flat."

"How soon does he need someone?" I tried hard to sound casual.

"By the end of the month. He hasn't advertised yet. Good jobs are hard to come by in the horse world and when he does there'll be hundreds after it. If you want to get in first, you'll have to be quick."

"But the end of the month is only two weeks away!" I said.

"Two weeks too long, I'd have thought." Forster thrust his foot into the liver chestnut's stirrup and swung himself into the saddle. At once the young entry were on their feet, sterns waving, ready to be off. Things were beginning to move rather too fast for me.

"But I've only just taken this job," I said in dismay. "I only started this morning!"

Forster shrugged. "So what? Hissey was out with us this morning and he'll be out again on Thursday. Do you want me to put a word in for you?"

"I don't know," I said, agonized. "I need time to think about it."

The liver chestnut sidled towards the clock arch, wanting to leave. Forster kicked it in the ribs. It obliged him by standing still and chucking its head up and down. "Listen Elaine," he said impatiently. "You've no prospects here. You haven't a hope in hell of earning a decent wage. If you pass up this opportunity, you're a fool."

"I know," I said. "It isn't that I don't want to take it. I do. But it's so sudden. I can't just walk out, not just like that. I should feel a cheat."

"The Fanes are not averse to a bit of cheating themselves," Forster said. He cuffed the liver chestnut's neck with his coiled whip. It stopped chucking its head and arched its neck, opened its mouth, and rattled the bit against its teeth.

"It isn't the Fanes I'm thinking about," I said miserably. "It's the horses."

I couldn't expect Forster to understand this. I only had to think of Nelson with his one eye and his hollow flanks, and the old bay mare with her gallant air and her dusty, threadbare coat, to feel a pull at my heart. And who would treat the black horse's thrush and school The Comet, if I didn't? And across the yard, Doreen's pony coughed and coughed and Brenda's cob with its pink nose and white eyelashes rested a footsore hind leg.

"You'll have to give me a little time to decide," I said. "I have to think things out."

"I'll ring you," Forster said. "On Wednesday night." He raised his whip in a salute and loosed his reins. The liver chestnut plunged across the yard. "By the way," he added, "you're very pretty." He disappeared under the clock arch and the young entry gambolled obediently after him without so much as a backward glance.

I went into the tackroom and I looked in the little spotted mirror on the wall. I couldn't see anything pretty. I saw my mother's pale blonde hair, but whereas hers had always been lightly permed and set into a distinctive style, mine hung straight to just below my ears and because I had cut it myself, it was a bit lopsided. My too pale skin was decorated with black splodges from the drains and my father's eyes stared back at me, grey and wide and rather vacant. Compared to the robust and colourful Fanes, I looked washed out and faded; I looked like a ghost. No, I saw nothing pretty in the tackroom mirror.

Hooves sounded and the Fanes clattered in from exercise, pink-cheeked and breathless, with cascades

51

of wind-blown hair. "We've just passed the young entry on the lane," Nigella gasped. "It was jolly bad luck that you were here by yourself. I bet Nick Forster was *hopping*."

"I hope you didn't let him get away with it, anyway," Henrietta said, sliding down the bad-tempered chestnut's shoulder. "I hope you gave as good as you got. It isn't as if it's *our* fault."

I took The Comet by his withered rein. "He wasn't all that angry," I said. "In fact, he was rather nice about it."

"Oh," Henrietta exclaimed in a knowing manner. "*Was* he!"

"I think we ought to warn you," Nigella said anxiously, "that he's not all that nice to know. He's got a terrible reputation."

"He's had an affair with half the county," Henrietta said, "including Mrs Lydia Lane, whose husband threatened to shoot him."

"And they do say," Nigella continued, "that he drinks rather more than he should."

"The Hissey groom was keen on him for ages," Henrietta said. "You wouldn't believe how badly he treated her. In the end, he was so insufferably awful to her at the Hunt Ball that she packed her cases and walked out."

"I see," I said. That explained why Forster had appeared so concerned about getting me a better job; it hadn't been done out of kindness, but because Felix Hissey had been left in the lurch, and Forster was responsible for it. I took the old bay mare by her bridle.

"I hope you don't think we are being prissy,"

Nigella said. "We're only telling you for your own good."

"After all," Henrietta added. "It's better to know these things. It's as well to have them pointed out."

"Thanks," I said. "I appreciate it."

I led The Comet and the old bay mare back to their stables. I had been up long before anyone else, and their beds were laid thick and clean and sweet, with banked up sides, scrubbed pails of clean water, and piles of newly shaken hay. The horses showed no surprise or gratification at their increased comfort, accepting it as their due. The satisfaction should have been mine. But somehow it wasn't. And it was all Forster's fault.

After that, the day went from bad to worse. Whilst the Fanes were out with the second lot of horses, I decided to ring the blacksmith. There was a dingy little room next to the kitchen which served as an office; if a wobbly table heaped with yellowing newspapers and copies of *Horse and Hound* dating back to the year dot, could be termed an office.

The office housed the telephone, and in my efforts to locate the local telephone directory, I pulled open the drawer in the table. It was stuffed with invoices. I might have closed it again if I hadn't noticed that one of them was from the blacksmith, and had his telephone number on the top. When I pulled it out, I noticed that it also had a little green sticker on the bottom saying YOUR CHEQUE WOULD OBLIGE. The next one I pulled out was of a more recent date and it had a different sort of sticker on it, a round one proclaiming THIS ACCOUNT IS OVERDUE in angry red letters. The next one was bigger altogether. It occupied a larger space and was edged in black. It threatened legal action if the account was not settled within ten days. The invoice was dated two weeks ago.

I sank down into a chair and looked through the invoices. There were dozens and dozens of them, not only from the blacksmith, but from the saddler, from the vet, from local farmers who had supplied hay and straw, and from the corn merchant. Some of them were almost a year old and none of them was receipted. They were all unpaid.

I knew now why the blacksmith hadn't been called, why the corn bins were empty and why the mineral supplement hadn't arrived. How could you call a blacksmith who was taking legal action to recover payment for past services? How could you place an order with a corn merchant who regretted that he must refuse any further credit and cease all future deliveries until the outstanding invoices were cleared?

I don't know how long I sat in that dismal little room, telling myself what a complete and utter fool, what a blind and crass idiot I had been. Asking myself how I had imagined, even for a minute, that by my own inept and inexperienced hand, I could salvage such an appallingly hopeless business.

My father had always numbered over-confidence and misplaced optimism amongst my prime failings. These defects, being completely alien to his own nature, he considered to be a character weakness inherited from my mother, a born optimist, who had left home for a man fifteen years her junior when I was ten. In view of this, it was hardly surprising that he should feel that pessimism and modesty were more solid attributes. Nevertheless, it didn't help to speculate how much he was going to enjoy being proved right again. How he would relish the opportunity of being able to say "*I told you so. Haven't I always told you that there is no future in horses.*"

Even Hans would have to smile to see me now. Just as he had smiled when I had outlined to him the plans I had made for my career, so tidily and confidently expounded, so forlornly and improvidently arranged. He had listened to me carefully, with his blond head slightly on one side, and one long, beautifully polished boot ledged in the bottom rail of the paddock fence. And when I had finished, he had sighed.

"So you think you go to an event yard, eh?" he had said. "You think you find a place to take you, with no trouble? And you think, even if it happens, that you are allowed to ride these event horses? You, with no experience at all? And you imagine that these kind people you find, because you work hard and they are pleased, that they let you compete on these horses, these good horses worth so many thousand of pounds? You think it will happen this easy?"

I had nodded. Standing there in all the euphoria of my newly awarded qualification, I had been sure that it would be.

But now I knew differently. And as I walked slowly up the dusty oak treads to my bedroom and started to repack my cases I was glad that Hans Gelderhol, The European Champion, The Golden Boy of Eventing, couldn't see me now.

5

Liquid Assets

I waited until the Fanes came into the kitchen for their tea. Then I told them I was leaving.

"*Leaving*?" Nigella said in tones of the very greatest astonishment. "But you have only just arrived!"

"I know," I said. "And I'm sorry. But I thought I could be useful. I really thought I would be able to cope."

"I knew she wouldn't stay," Henrietta exclaimed. She turned to Nigella in exasperation. "Didn't I tell you she wouldn't? Didn't I warn you that she was just using us as a stopgap? Only taking our job until she found something better?"

"I'm not leaving because I've found something better," I said. "I haven't found another job. I haven't anything else in mind at all." This was true. I had considered applying for the job with Felix Hissey and I had decided against it. For one thing I didn't want to get involved with Nick Forster and his sordid affairs, and for another I hadn't the face to take a job where I would be bumping into the Fanes every five minutes. Then there were the horses. I had to steel myself not to think about them. I had made up my mind that the only thing to do was to make a clean break. I had to leave the area; to creep back home with my tail between my legs; to start again, scanning the *Situations Vacant*. The prospect was depressing, to say the least.

"But if you haven't found another job; if you haven't anywhere else to go," Nigella said, mystified, "why are you leaving?"

"I'm leaving because things are worse than I ever imagined," I said. "I'm leaving because of *these*." I threw the sheaf of unpaid invoices on to the kitchen table.

The Fanes stared at them in silence.

"Oh," Henrietta said eventually in a flat voice. "Those."

"You can't run a yard without money," I said. "No one can. You have to pay the bills. You didn't tell me you were bankrupt."

"We are not exactly bankrupt," Nigella said in her careful way. "At least," she added, "not yet."

"Where did you find them, anyway?" Henrietta demanded indignantly. "We didn't employ you to pry into our private affairs. Or to search through our drawers."

"I was looking for a telephone directory," I said wearily. "I wanted to ring the blacksmith."

"I'm rather glad you didn't," Nigella said with a hollow little laugh. "He would have been awfully cross."

"I'm the one who's entitled to be cross," I pointed out. "You should never have employed me. You can't afford to employ anyone. I wonder you even had the nerve to place the advertisement. No wonder you wouldn't discuss my wages."

"You're not entitled to any wages yet," Henrietta flared. "You've hardly done anything!"

Nigella picked up the invoices. She flipped through them in a desultory manner. "They do seem to have built up a bit," she admitted. "But I expect we will manage to pay them off. After all, the hunting season is almost here, and there will be money coming in from the hirelings and the liveries. You said so yourself."

"Hirelings have to be fed," I reminded her. "They also need to be shod. And your liveries are leaving."

"What do you mean our liveries are leaving?" Henrietta cried. "That's a lie!"

"It isn't a lie," I said. "I saw Doreen and Brenda this morning. They told me." After the traumatic visit of the young entry I had completely forgotten to mention it.

"They don't *mean* it," Nigella said. "They keep on saying it. They just use it as a threat. But they would never actually *leave*. I'm sure of it."

"They do mean it," I said. "They've given you a week to get the blacksmith and the mineral supplement. Otherwise," I added, remembering Brenda's words, "they're off."

"That's blackmail," Henrietta muttered. "They've no right."

"They've every right," I said.

Nigella put the invoices back on to the table. "Things are pretty bad," she said. "We may as well admit it."

I wondered if she realized quite how bad things were. "In a week," I said, "the oats will be gone altogether. In a week there won't be a horse left in the yard with a full set of shoes on."

"It won't worry you," Henrietta snapped, "since you won't be here."

"In a week," I said, "you won't have any hay left at all."

There was a silence in which Nigella stared at the

invoices in a distressed manner, and Henrietta picked angrily at her sleeve which was unravelled almost as far as the elbow. I told myself that I shouldn't feel emotional about it. There was nothing I could do. It wasn't my problem. I blinked hard and studied a sepia photograph on the kitchen wall. Under the fly blown glass, Lady Jennifer, willow-slim and elegant, posed her hunter for posterity. Something about the horse was familiar. I looked closer and I saw that it was the old bay mare, fit and sleek and in her prime. The photograph was pasted to a piece of cardboard scattered with thunder flies, and in one of the lower corners there was some writing in faded ink. "Little Legend" it said, "1947". The old bay mare was nearly forty years old.

I stared at the photograph and I wondered when she had stopped being Little Legend and become just the old bay mare. It didn't take much imagination to picture the steady decline of the stables, to know that every year there would have been less to spend and less people to care. Like a gallant old pensioner, the old bay mare had weathered the hard times. She had lost her comfort, her youth and her looks, but she still had her spirit. She deserved a better end.

"Nigella," I said. "If there was some way; if things were not quite so hopeless, I wouldn't leave."

"I know," she said, "and there is a way."

Henrietta looked up from her elbow. "Which way is that?" she enquired in a suspicious tone.

"We shall have to sell something," Nigella said. "Although to be honest, there is not a lot left."

"Well, don't look at me," Henrietta said. "I only have my secretaire; and I'm not selling."

"Then it will have to be my vases," Nigella decided.

Selling the vases meant that I had to drive the shooting brake to London. I had passed my driving test before I left the training centre, but since then I had not driven at all. My father flatly refused to allow me behind the wheel of his beloved Morris Minor. It was his most cherished possession and he was very proud of the fact that it was still in the same gleamingly pristine condition as when he had driven it out of the showroom twenty years ago. So I was a bit alarmed at the thought of having to face the London traffic with a valuable cargo of vases.

The next morning, after a herculean effort in the stables and a shortened form of communal exercise, we peeled off our anoraks and wellingtons and rushed upstairs to change into town clothes. It only took me a few seconds to flip through the hangers in the wormy, carved wardrobe and realize that I hadn't anything resembling town clothes with me at all. I couldn't even find a clean shirt. I flew along the passage to tell Nigella and bumped into Henrietta, who was already changed. She had added fluorescent purple socks and scuffed pink spikey-heeled shoes to her awful drainpipe jeans and topped it all with a horrific moth-eaten fur coat with padded shoulders. She didn't look as if she had even combed her hair.

After that I settled for jeans and a roll-necked jersey under my hacking jacket which made a nice rustic contrast to Nigella, who appeared in something that looked suspiciously like a pink openwork bedjacket which tied at the neck with a grubby piece

60

of satin ribbon, the inevitable drainpipes and red tap-dancing shoes.

I set off gingerly down the drive, steering the shooting brake in and out of the pot-holes, trying to avoid the bumps. The Fanes sat nursing the vases on the back seat.

"Heavens," Henrietta grumbled. "I hope you're not going to drive like this all the way to town. Can't you drive in a straight line?"

"You're jolly lucky I can drive at all," I pointed out. "It wasn't a requirement of the job. It wasn't mentioned in the advert."

"Quite a lot of things weren't mentioned in the advert," Nigella remarked, cranking down her window to dispose of some withered dahlias which had been sitting in the neck of her vase. "It's a bit of a sore point."

None of my previous driving experience, not even suffering brake failure after stalling the land rover whilst ferrying Hans round the cross-country course, had prepared me for the terrors of negotiating the London traffic. It was fearful.

The Fanes were no help. Whilst I was being honked and hustled and trapped in the wrong lanes, narrowly avoiding being rammed by taxi cabs or mown down by buses, they yelped and clutched their vases and bounced up and down in their seats, shouting out conflicting directions as to the quickest way to get to Knightsbridge.

Finally, after whirling round and round a one-way system in a state of near hysteria, we arrived at an underground carpark. There was a portable sign blocking the entrance saying FULL. In a trice, Nigella was out of the shooting brake and had heaved the sign aside.

"Drive on in," Henrietta commanded. "We shall have to bribe someone to find us a space."

I drove into the gloom and almost knocked over the attendant who was hot-foot after the person who had removed his sign. He leapt aside and banged angrily on the roof with his fist. I stamped on the brake, released the clutch and stalled the shooting brake. Henrietta, who was holding both vases, shot forward in her seat and screamed, and Nigella, who was coming along behind, walked into the rear doors.

The attendant took advantage of the confusion and grabbed Nigella by her bedjacket, demanding to know what she thought she was up to, moving his sign. Full was full, he said. And that meant every-body. It took Nigella quite a while to calm him down, but eventually she tripped round the front of the shooting brake and stuck her head in at my window.

"Has anyone got any money?" she enquired.

There was a silence.

"He says he'll do it for a pound," she said urgently. "If we leave the car unlocked and the keys in the ignition, he'll move it into the first vacant space."

The attendant leered at us. Regretfully I handed over my last pound coin. I was not too sure when or if I would ever see another.

We took it in turns to carry the vases through the streets. They were very large. They were also very heavy. They had fat bulbous bodies and little thin necks with nasty little handles shaped like ears attached to them. Not only that but they were decorated all over with ladies and butterflies and trelliswork in vivid shapes of gold and burnt umber. They were the most hideous vases I had seen in the whole of my life. I couldn't imagine that anyone could possibly want to buy them.

We turned into the main entrance to Harrods and stepped on to the escalator.

"Nigella," I said as we sailed majestically upwards. "What if they don't *want* them?"

Nigella was standing in front of me with her hands clasped round the belly of her vase and its neck lodged under her chin. "It'll be all right," she said in a muffled voice. "Honestly."

"Of course they'll *want* them," Henrietta interposed from behind in an acid voice. "We've been dealing with Harrods for years. We should know what they want by now."

When it seemed that we could go up no further, we stepped off the escalator and began to weave our way through an endless maze of tapestry armchairs. At the end of it all there was a glittering chandelier, an empty suit of armour, and the entrance to the Fine Arts Department.

Almost as soon as we had stepped inside, the Fine Arts Gentleman came hurrying over. He eyed the vases with obvious pleasure and ushered us into an inner sanctum. He seemed to be an old friend.

"What is it this time?" he said, relieving us of the vases and placing them reverently on a baize-topped table. "Central heating perhaps? Or a winter holiday in the Canaries?"

"No such luck," Nigella said. "We need to refurbish the stables. The cost is horrendous."

"I can imagine." The Fine Arts Gentleman pulled out an immaculately folded handkerchief on which to polish his eyeglass. "Provenance?" he enquired.

Henrietta rummaged in the pockets of her verminous fur coat and handed him a screwed up piece of paper. He smoothed it out carefully on the table and studied it.

"They've been in the family for two hundred years at least," Nigella said. "They're Cantonese. They are supposed to be rather valuable."

"They are indeed," the Fine Arts Gentleman agreed. "They are an extremely fine pair of Cantonese porcelain baluster vases. Circa 1780, unless I am very much mistaken." He screwed in his eyeglass and turned one of the vases upside down in order to examine the base. A thick brown soup rolled slowly out of the neck, down his trouser leg, over his beautiful suede shoes, and spread in a glutinous pool on the carpet. The inner sanctum was suddenly filled with the most disgusting smell.

"Oh!" Nigella gasped in dismay. "Mummy's dahlia water!"

The Fine Arts Gentleman recoiled, catching his breath.

"We're most terribly, awfully sorry," Nigella cried. She tried to mop up some of the soup with a paper handkerchief. It was thick and slimy. I thought that if I didn't go outside, I should probably be sick. Henrietta had already backed away as far as the door and had her hand clamped across her mouth.

When the Fine Arts Gentleman had recovered himself sufficiently, he paid us £2,000 for the vases. It wasn't quite enough to pay all the bills, but it was enough to get us out of trouble. On the way home, Henrietta composed a little song to mark the occasion. It was the first time I had heard her sing. She was surprisingly good.

6

Thunder and Lightning

A few days later we were in the thick of preparations for hunting, when Nigella came back from the post-box at the end of the drive, gleefully waving a letter.

"It's in reply to our advertisement," she shouted. "Come and see!"

The Fanes had placed another advertisement in *Horse and Hound*, but this time I had been allowed to compose it.

Small High Class Livery Yard in the Midvale and Westbury Hunt Country (I had put) *has a few vacancies for the coming season. Apply: Havers Hall, Westbury, Suffolk.*

There had been little point in adding a telephone number since our line had been disconnected. There hadn't been enough money left to buy clippers *and* pay the telephone account, and the clippers had seemed more important. We were desperate to attract more liveries because we needed a regular source of income; the vases had bought us time, but already the bills were building up again.

At the time of the letter, Henrietta and I were engaged in clipping the black horse. It was no easy task. Backed into a corner and held firmly by the nose and a foreleg, we managed to make him stand fast, but he soon discovered that if he put his mind to it, he could send ripples along his skin like wind through winter wheat. It slowed up the clipping considerably, and the motor had begun to overheat. We were glad of a break.

Henrietta released the black horse who immediately shook himself like a dog and began to sag at the knees as a preliminary to getting down in the box for a good roll. We thwarted him by tying him to the hayrack. I threw a blanket over his naked hindquarters and we left him to have a good fidget whilst we went up to the house to investigate the letter.

Nigella was in the kitchen making coffee. The letter was lying on the table. I picked it up. It was typed on thick, cream paper and there was a business heading at the top. "THUNDER AND LIGHTNING LIMITED" it said, and underneath there was an address in Clapham.

"It's obviously a double glazing firm," Nigella said in a jubilant tone. "One of the very best. You only have to look at the paper: it's embossed." She chipped enthusiastically at a lump of solidified sugar and dropped the bits into our mugs. There weren't any biscuits; we had no time for cookery.

"Read it out, read it out," Henrietta said impatiently jiggling my elbow. "Don't keep it all to yourself."

Dear Sirs (I read),
Having noticed your recent advertisement in *Horse and Hound* I am writing to enquire if it would be possible for you to take three hunters at full livery for the coming season? Owing to the nature and timing of our engagements, we are not able to hunt more than two or three times a month, but my colleagues and I have found it unsatisfactory to hire horses in the past.

Should you have a vacancy, I would be grateful if you would quote your terms, in order that we may come to a decision as soon as possible.

Yours faithfully,

J P Jones

pp. Thunder and Lightning Limited.

"Glory," Henrietta gasped. She sat down on a kitchen chair with a thump. "Three liveries! *Three*."

"And business types," Nigella said gloatingly. "Exactly the sort you wanted, Elaine. High class liveries, to add tone to the yard."

"We had better write back," Henrietta said, becoming agitated. "*Immediately*. They may have written to other places. We must get in first." She ran into the office and began to search frantically for notepaper and a pen.

"Sit down Elaine," Nigella said. "You must write our reply. And I will post it when I go out with the second lot of horses." She sat beside me and looked expectant. Henrietta managed to unearth a clean sheet of notepaper with the family crest in one corner, and a ball point pen which turned out to be red. This necessitated another search. Finally I was able to begin.

Dear Mr Jones (I wrote),

Thank you for your enquiry. I am pleased to confirm that we have sufficient vacancies to accommodate your three hunter liveries for the coming season . . .

"That's good," Nigella said appreciatively. "That's really good."

I also have pleasure in quoting our terms, which are as follows:

I looked up at the Fanes. "What are our terms?" I said.

Henrietta shrugged her shoulders in a vague sort of way.

"We don't actually have any set terms," Nigella said. "So you can put what you like."

"You must have some idea of what you charge," I said. "What about Doreen? What about Brenda?"

"Ah," Nigella said uneasily. "They have been here a long time."

"They pay for their own foodstuffs," Henrietta pointed out. "They pay the blacksmith, and they do all their own exercising."

"All the same," I said, "I would like to know what they pay."

"Actually," Nigella admitted. "It's five pounds."

I was astounded by this piece of information. The rent of the stable alone was worth five pounds a week, and the Fanes had been supplying hay and straw, not to mention the labour involved in mucking out and feeding.

"You're crazy," I told them. "You're absolutely mad. You deserve to be bankrupt."

"If we had charged more, they might have found somewhere cheaper," Nigella protested. "Then we wouldn't have had anybody."

"And ten pounds a week in cash," Henrietta added, "is very handy."

"Ten pounds a week for two liveries," I said crossly, "is *pathetic*."

"All right," Henrietta said, nettled. "If you think you are so jolly clever, *you* fix the livery rates."

"You are quite right, of course," Nigella said hastily. "We haven't been charging enough. You had better adjust the prices, Elaine. We are completely in your hands; make it ten, if you like."

I turned my attention back to the letter. There was no point in starting an argument. When it came to costing, the Fanes were hopeless. They hadn't a clue.

Full Livery (I wrote) £25 per week
Shoeing and Veterinary Fees extra.

"Twenty-five pounds," Nigella gasped. "For a week!"

"They won't pay it," Henrietta said in a scandalized voice. "Twenty-five pounds for a livery is far too expensive. Honestly Elaine, sometimes I wonder whose side you are on. This may be our one chance to make a success of the yard, and you are going to price us out of business!"

"Twenty-five pounds a week is reasonable," I said firmly. "At the training centre, the hunter liveries paid thirty-five."

"But we are not the training centre," Nigella said. "We haven't the staff for one thing, or the facilities."

"And we're fed up with hearing about the training centre," Henrietta said. "We find it very boring."

"And I find you very boring," I snapped. "I thought you wanted to run a high class yard? I thought you wanted to attract quality liveries?"

"We do," Henrietta said in a grumpy voice. "You know we do."

"We are only being cautious," Nigella pointed out. "We are not trying to be difficult."

"If we agree to charge twenty-five pounds," Henrietta said, "what about Brenda? What about Doreen?"

"Their rates will have to go up as well," I said. "And if they don't like it, they will have to move out."

"I realize that we have to be economic," Nigella sighed, "but it does seem a bit hard. After all, they are old clients; and Brenda is sure to take it badly. She can be very difficult."

"You can leave Brenda and Doreen to me," I said. "If they want to stay, they can have their livery at a slightly reduced rate. Brenda is no fool, she must know how much it would cost to keep her horse elsewhere. We are not going to be a cut price establishment."

"Better a full cut price establishment," Henrietta grumbled, "than an empty high class one."

"It didn't take you long to foul things up, Busy Bee," Brenda commented when I told her that her livery had gone up to twenty pounds, but as a concession to her long residence she would no longer have to pay for her own foodstuffs. "I thought something like this was in the wind. Well, I can't say things haven't improved, so I expect I shall have to cough up; but Doreen won't. She's only a kid. She won't be able to afford it."

"I've thought about Doreen," I said. "Her livery is only a pony, so it won't cost so much. It doesn't need the corn for one thing. I thought we would charge her fourteen pounds a week, and as she likes to hang around the yard perhaps she could help out sometimes, in the evenings perhaps, or at weekends.

71

If we paid her a pound an hour, we could deduct it from her livery bill. We could do with an extra hand, and it isn't as if she would have to do it all the year round; her pony goes out to grass in the spring."

"I've got to hand it to you, Busy Bee," Brenda said grudgingly. "You've got all the answers."

The Fanes, who were secretly terrified of Brenda, were much impressed with these negotiations, but they were alarmed at the thought of having to pay Doreen a pound an hour. They were slightly mollified when I explained that they would not actually be required to hand over hard cash, which was something they were incredibly mean about and would go to inordinate lengths to avoid. As soon as there was some regular income coming into the yard I meant to pin them down on the subject of my pocket money wages. There was no point in mentioning it until then, because the Fanes were as broke as I was.

We didn't get any more replies from the advertisement, so we were more than a bit anxious about the response to our letter to Thunder and Lightning Limited. Every day Nigella ran down to the postbox at the end of the drive and every day she returned with another bill we couldn't pay. But there was no reply to our letter.

"I told you twenty-five pounds was too much," Henrietta said bitterly. "I told you they wouldn't pay it."

"If they can't afford twenty-five pounds a week," I retorted, "we don't want them anyway." But even I began to wonder if I had pitched our prices too high to start with; that maybe we would have been better to start low and fill the yard as Henrietta had maintained.

One morning when Nigella came back from the postbox there was a letter for me. It was from my father. Now that I had landed a job which had lasted all of a fortnight, and rather more especially, I suspected, because the Fanes had a title and a grand-sounding address, he had softened in his attitude. He was prepared to come to visit me.

This change of heart was something of a mixed blessing. Whilst I was pleased to think that at last my father might be beginning to accept my choice of career, I was vastly alarmed at the prospect of having to introduce him to the Fanes. I knew that Havers Hall and its occupants would not be quite what he expected. Also, that seeing me in such down-at-heel circumstances, he would immediately smell exploitation and demand to know how much I was being paid in wages, if I was covered by Employers' Liability Insurance, if my National Insurance Contributions were being paid, and a dozen other niggling little details he considered important. To further complicate matters, the date he had suggested for his intended visit was the day we had planned to take some of the horses cubbing, as a pipe-opener for the opening meet. It was all very inconvenient.

I mentioned the last problem to Nigella who, with her customary tact, said that I should on no account try to put him off, for fear of causing offence.

"He doesn't want to come until mid-morning anyway," she pointed out. "And as the meet is at eight-thirty, you could leave early and be back by then. When they meet in the village, they always end up by drawing the edge of the park, so it isn't as

73

if you will be far away. And Mummy will be home, it isn't her Meals-on-Wheels day and she would be delighted to meet your father."

Mummy was delighted. Lady Jennifer immediately identified my father as a Good Cause.

"But *Elaine*," she shrilled. "How simply *marvellous*! Of course your father must pay us a visit. I shall be absolutely *thrilled* to entertain him."

The day before the entertainment was due to take place she bucketed down to the village store in the shooting brake and returned with a box of livid iced fancies and a packet of custard creams which, in the Fane household, represented the height of extravagance.

I hadn't the heart to tell her that my father refused to eat commercially produced confections of any kind because he was convinced that the white sugar they contained poisoned the system.

7

A Friend of a Friend

The cubbing morning was dry and bright, with just the right amount of autumnal nip in the air. The meet was at the Westbury crossroads, which meant that we could hack there.

Our party consisted of Nigella on the mare-who-sometimes-slipped-a-stifle, Henrietta on the black-horse-who-never-stood-still, myself on the bad-tempered chestnut, and Doreen, who because her pony had not completely recovered from its cough had been allowed to take the old bay mare. There was also a solitary client, a Mr McLoughlin, described by Lady Jennifer as a friend of a friend, who after much deliberation had been allocated The Comet, the only horse in the stable who was up to weight.

To our consternation, when he arrived, Mr McLoughlin turned out to be small and spindly and not very experienced. However, there was no time to do anything about it and he professed himself overwhelmed to be presented with The Comet who, clipped and newly shod, with a neatly pulled mane and tail, looked a picture.

Now that there were three of us and Doreen working in the yard, the horses were beginning to look reasonably presentable. They were still rather too lean, especially the old bay mare, whose age was against her, and Nelson. Nelson had found having his jaw put in a metal clamp and a file rasped along his back teeth up to his eye sockets an alarming experience. He had spent the rest of the day rattling his mouth in the water bucket, which by evening stables was topped with froth and lined with tooth chippings. The next morning, though, he had cheered up and when I went into his stable I found him standing on bare brick; during the night he had not only eaten his corn feed and his hay net, but also his bedding. I had high hopes of Nelson.

The black horse still looked like a racehorse after the Derby. His nervous energy would never allow him to maintain any condition, but his thrush was drying up, his coat was glossy, and he had a certain dashing attraction that captured the eye. The Comet, the bad-tempered chestnut, and the mare-who-sometimes-slipped-a-stifle all looked smart and well-covered. They were not one hundred per cent fit by any means, and they lacked muscle, especially behind the saddle, but I couldn't help feeling pleased as we set out in the watery sunshine with our breath hanging in the air like smoke, the horses bright-eyed and well shod, and the saddlery, even if it was not new or even very modern, soaped and, thanks to Nigella's hideous vases, mended and safe.

The only dubious note was struck by the Fanes themselves who didn't appear to possess any riding garments other than the drainpipe jeans. Even so, with the addition of old-fashioned leather riding boots with laces up the front, baggy tweed costume jackets which probably originated from the Oxfam Shop, and their hair in long plaits beneath their bowler hats, they achieved a certain period charm; all the same, I hoped that they would manage something rather better for the opening meet.

Hounds were already waiting at the crossroads when we arrived; the black horse went into a *Piaffe* at the sight of them. The Master, a round, red-faced man with a waxed moustache, wished us a cheery good morning as we clattered up, and the Huntsman, who looked lean, hungry and irritated, favoured us with a curt nod. The rest of the field consisted of two middle-aged women on big raw-boned thorough-breds, a boy on a piebald cob, and a tall, thin, nervous-looking man on a threequarter-bred bay gelding.

Nigella, Doreen, Mr McLoughlin and I stood our horses quietly in the lane a little way apart from the others. The black horse fussed and fidgeted about and arched his neck and swished his tail. His neck and shoulders were already patched with sweat. Mr McLoughlin, with his stirrups too short and his toes pointing firmly towards the ground, seemed to be perfectly happy and confident on The Comet, leaning forward every now and again to clap him affectionately on the neck. I had ridden The Comet out to exercise several times and I had found him an obedient and intelligent horse, if at times rather world-weary in his attitude. At some time in his life someone had schooled him with great care and I found it hard to reconcile this with the Fanes' assertions that he was a confirmed bolter. If this was so, he had yet to show his true colours.

"I wonder if the pups are out," Nigella said. She stood up in her stirrups, scanning the pack for familiar faces. "The trouble is that when they are all together, it's nearly impossible to tell them apart."

William and Forster were holding up hounds on

the little grass triangle in the middle of the cross-roads. When William saw us, his jaw dropped and he stared at the horses in open astonishment. After that, when he wasn't paying attention to hounds, he stared at Henrietta instead. Henrietta ignored him. Forster on the other hand, immaculately mounted on a grey, hardly gave us a glance. But when one of the young entry recognized Nigella's voice and came gambolling across the lane to greet us, he kicked his horse after it and sent it scuttling back.

He lifted his hat to the Fanes. I hoped with all my heart that he wouldn't say anything about the job. I felt myself grow hot and I lifted my saddle flap and fumbled with the straps, pretending to tighten my girth.

"I tried to ring you on Wednesday," Forster said. "There seemed to be something wrong with the telephone."

"We've got a faulty line," Henrietta said smartly. "It's a cable fault."

"Is that so?" Forster gave her a cool look. "The operator seemed to think you had been disconnected."

Henrietta shot him a glance of pure hatred before being carried out of earshot by the black horse, who was executing a *passage*.

"I take it that you've decided against the job," Forster said, "otherwise you would have let me know."

"Yes," I said. "I would . . . I mean, I have . . . and if you wouldn't mind, I would rather not discuss it." I felt hatefully embarrassed. Forster had kept his voice low so that the others wouldn't hear, but all conversation had stopped and I knew everyone was staring. My face had turned scarlet.

Forster seemed to find it very amusing, it was obviously the kind of situation he enjoyed. "I shall have to come and visit you at the Hall," he said, and this time he didn't trouble to keep his voice down. "I'm sure Lady Jennifer won't object."

Nigella gave me a startled look. I opened my mouth to protest but I was saved from having to reply by the bad-tempered chestnut who, realizing that my hands had turned to jelly on the reins, took advantage of the situation to dive forward with flattened ears in order to sink his yellow teeth into the neck of Forster's grey.

The grey horse shot backwards in dismay and bumped one of the thoroughbreds, who began to spin round like a top, lashing out at everything in sight. The tall, thin, nervous man's horse leapt in the air and catapulted him out of the saddle on to the lane. In the resulting confusion, Nigella and I sought the refuge of the grass verge where the rest of our party had collected.

"Serve him right," Henrietta commented in a valedictory tone. "Ought to have been *his* neck."

Soon afterwards, the Master decided it was time to move off. We followed hounds along the lane and across a track towards the first covert. The tall, thin, nervous man rode in front of us, holding his horse tightly and shouting at it. The horse was upset and refused to walk; it pranced along unhappily and kept shaking its head, making the man more nervous than ever.

"I do wish people wouldn't overmount themselves," Nigella said in a low voice. "He'll ruin that

79

lovely animal; not only that, but he'll frighten himself to death at the same time."

"I'll keep an eye on him," Henrietta promised. "If the horse has him off again, I shall offer him fifty pounds for it. He'll probably be only too pleased to accept."

At the first few coverts of the day there was not a lot of action; as it was so close to the new season, the hunt didn't want to cull the cubs, just scatter them. We were told to ring the coverts with orders not to send the cubs back, but to let them get away. The coverts seemed to be full of foxes. They ran out everywhere, streaking away across stubble and plough, whilst hounds blundered about in the undergrowth. At one point, a young fox ran straight between the black horse's front legs, causing him to go totally rigid for at least a minute. It was, Henrietta declared, the longest she had ever known him to stand still on his own account.

As a reward for scattering the cubs, the Master informed us that we could expect a run at the next draw if hounds were diligent enough to put out an old dog fox who had given good sport for three seasons without losing a hair of his brush. The draw was a long straggling copse and we were positioned at set intervals on the ride that surrounded it, each person out of sight and sound of the others. The draw was planned like a military operation and everyone was given a part to play, something that is never possible after the opening meet, with fields of hundreds for the Master to control.

I was sent to watch a triangle of scrub at the end of the copse, which finished in a vast field of plough, stretching off into the sky, speckled with gulls and pewits. The bad-tempered chestnut and I stood on the ride, listening. The silence was total.

Nothing happened for ages and just as I had decided that nothing ever would, and even the bad-tempered chestnut had lost interest and was chewing a twig, I heard the Huntsman's voice. There were some rustlings and cracklings and a, "Leu in there, try over," followed by a yelp. Then a hound spoke inside the copse and almost immediately another joined in. The bad-tempered chestnut stiffened to attention, his ears pointed forward like a terrier.

A few seconds later there was a holloa, a shrill, spine-tingling scream along the ride, and almost simultaneously Forster steamed past, galloping hard, with a couple of hounds at his horse's heels. After a moment's hesitation I followed. Flying round the edge of the copse, the bad-tempered chestnut and I suddenly came across Henrietta standing in the middle of the ride, holding her hat in the air.

"Don't come any further," she shouted. "Don't cross the line!"

The bad-tempered chestnut applied his brakes and skidded to a halt. The black horse, knowing there was to be a run, was in an agony of impatience, plunging and dancing all over the ride and frothing at the mouth. It was all Henrietta could do to hold him with one hand. Suddenly there was a staccato burst on the horn and the entire pack flashed across the ride between us. The Huntsman crashed after them, cheering them on. The black horse leapt in the air and carried Henrietta after them even before she had time to cram her hat back on to her head.

The bad-tempered chestnut and I followed at a more cautious pace. I wanted to be sure that hounds were all out of the copse and that the Hunt Staff had got away first. I didn't want to find myself galloping in the middle of the pack and in front of the Master on my first day out.

By the time we had negotiated the headland of the plough, the rest of our party had joined us and hounds were strung out two fields ahead. It was marvellous to be riding across country again. The bad-tempered chestnut didn't have much scope because he was a small, compact horse with a naturally short stride; but he was very game. He tackled everything that came his way. He slithered down and scrambled up the sides of ditches the bigger horses took in one massive flying leap; he shrugged his way through brambles and undergrowth the thin-skinned blood horses baulked at; and he laboured manfully over the plough. Whenever we hit grass or stubble, he showed a surprising turn of speed. Galloping along with the wind stinging my face, the chestnut neck stretched in front of me, and the regular thud of hooves beneath me, I felt alive again for the first time since I had left the training centre.

Another dozen or more riders joined the field as the morning wore on. Hounds had begun to slow down and were swinging in a wide circle when I looked at my watch and realized that it was time to leave. Punctuality was one of my father's strong points and I knew he wouldn't be even a minute late. I pushed the bad-tempered chestnut on slightly to catch up with Nigella, who was riding slightly in front. Doreen and the old bay mare were well behind but I could see the black horse and The Comet almost two fields ahead, practically level with the

Master. Mr McLoughlin was by no means being run away with; his reins were lying loose upon The Comet's neck, his seat was waving in the air, and he was having the ride of his life; worth every penny of the twenty pounds I intended to charge him.

"Can't you stay a little longer?" Nigella gasped, when we were stirrup to stirrup and I had shouted that I was about to leave. She added something about turning for home anyway and having to watch The Comet, but I lost most of it in the rattle of hooves as we dropped off a bank into a narrow lane. The lane seemed a good place to make the break, so I pulled up and set off for home. The bad-tempered chestnut was as reluctant as I was to leave when hounds were running. He clamped his tail to his rump, fixed his ears back and sulked.

Along the lane we came upon the tall, thin man struggling to load the bay horse into his trailer. The horse was rearing and rolling its eyes and the man was shouting and hitting it with the end of the headcollar rope. I dismounted and stood behind the horse, slapping its hindquarters and making encouraging noises and the bad-tempered chestnut did what he could by snaking out his head and snapping his teeth, and eventually the bay horse went up the ramp. As I fastened the breeching, the tall, thin man told me that the bay horse was only on trial, and that, by jove, it was off back the first thing in the morning; he couldn't wait to see the last of it. I was relieved to hear it because the bay horse was far too high couraged for him, it deserved better than the tall, thin man; and I knew that he would be a different person on a more suitable horse. He wasn't cruel, only frightened; but fright can make even a timid man into a tyrant where horses are concerned.

By the time I had mounted up again and reached the Hall, it was a quarter past eleven and my father was due to arrive at half past. I rubbed down the bad-tempered chestnut, rugged him up and left him warm and dry with his mash and his hay and dashed up to the house. There was just time to jump in and out of a luke-warm bath, which was the best the hot water system could achieve, to drag on some clean clothes and to clatter downstairs where I found Lady Jennifer laying out the iced fancies and the custard creams in her own little sitting room.

The sitting room was the only furnished reception room in the house and it was enhanced by Henrietta's Vile secretaire. Lady Jennifer was all prepared for tea with an electric kettle sitting on the hearth, together with a teapot with the silver plate rubbed off, and some china cups and plates of assorted design. A single bar electric fire only just failed to banish the chill from the air. It was not quite gracious living, but I was touched and grateful. I only hoped my father would be.

At exactly half past eleven we were hovering by the front door and we heard the sound of a car on the drive. I felt incredibly nervous. I was almost glad that my father had chosen a hunting day to visit. At least, with the Fane sisters out of the way, the setting was serene. And Lady Jennifer, as she swept down the stone steps in her ancient tweeds with her hair pinned into an untidy bun, looked the picture of impoverished gentry.

The immaculate Morris Minor came to a careful halt and my father got out and gave me a perfunctory kiss on the cheek. I was just beginning to introduce him to Lady Jennifer when there was a wild shriek from somewhere in the park.

As we turned towards it, we heard thundering hooves and a riderless horse came into view with reins and stirrups flying. The horse was The Comet and he was heading for the stables at full speed. Lady Jennifer barely had time to grip my arm with her bony fingers, when three couple of hounds, sopping wet from the river, burst through the remains of the yew hedge and hurled themselves upon us with yelps of joy. My father, with admirable presence of mind, opened the door of the Morris Minor to take refuge, but before he could set foot inside, one of the young entry beat him to it and seated itself proudly upon the driver's seat, awaiting the inevitable transport back to the kennels.

All this happened in an instant and it was followed up by the arrival of the old bay mare with Doreen aboard, hatless, her hair flopping over her eyes and her cheeks pink with exertion. They cleared the yew hedge in fine style and almost landed on top of us.

"We tried to turn them," Doreen shrieked. "But Mr McLoughlin hit a tree!" She hauled furiously at the old bay mare to prevent herself being conveyed back to the yard and kicked her wildly in the ribs. "He's lying in the park! Felled like an ox and as dead as a doorknob!"

Lady Jennifer, who throughout this recital had been crying, "Oh! Oh!" in dismay, now turned deathly pale and set off at a run for the park gate, dragging my father with her. I jumped up behind Doreen, but the old bay mare refused to jump back over the hedge with an extra passenger and after a few nerve-racking tries, we abandoned the idea and made for the gate as well.

In the event, Mr McLoughlin was not dead. He had risen from the spot where he had been felled by an overhanging bough whilst grappling with The Comet's iron will, and he was tottering towards us. His bowler hat was broken, there was blood flowing from his brow, and his breeches were streaked with grass stains. As Lady Jennifer loosed hold of my father and rushed to support him, the hunt swept past us like the Charge of the Light Brigade on the trail of the old dog fox who was heading for the certain safety of the plantation. With the ground vibrating under our feet, we made for the park railings where, just as we were engaged in heaving Mr McLoughlin over the top, more galloping hooves, whip crackings, and some colourful old English language heralded the arrival of William, red hot with temper over the desertion of his hounds.

All of this was like a nightmare. When we got back to the Morris Minor it was packed with hounds. The upholstery was soaked and steam was coming out of the open door. Noses were pressed expectantly against the windows. The Comet, who had returned to his stable only to find the lower door closed against him, paced up and down the drive looking anxious. He had broken his reins.

Somehow I managed to push the young entry out of the car. They took one sideways look at William's whip, tucked their sterns between their legs and fled across the park towards the plantation.

My father and I faced each other across the ruined upholstery. His tie was askew and his good suit was patched with damp. Mr McLoughlin's blood was on his cheek and his hair was standing up in a crest. To one side of us, Lady Jennifer was supporting the injured party, who appeared to be deliberating as to whether he should remount The Comet. Doreen and the old bay mare were engaged in a private battle, churning up the gravel.

My father, who prided himself on being articulate and erudite, could find no words to suit the occasion. When he did speak it was in a voice stupefied by the passage of events.

"Elaine," he said faintly. "My *dear* child."

8

Eventer's Dream

Mr McLoughlin was persuaded not to remount, which was a great relief to everyone. He seemed to feel that he might lose his nerve if he didn't get back into the saddle right away, but Lady Jennifer assured him that this was nothing but an old wives' tale, and Doreen was allowed to lead The Comet and the old bay mare back to the stables.

When the friend of a friend had been conveyed to a bathroom to be cleaned off, and a sticking plaster had been applied to his head, he got out his wallet.

"No, no," Lady Jennifer cried, aghast. "Put it away! We wouldn't *dream* of charging you for such a *ghastly* experience. We couldn't *bear* to take any fee whatsoever!"

This foiled my plan somewhat, because I had been quite prepared to charge him twenty pounds, having decided that falls and minor injuries were an integral part of the chase. But Mr McLoughlin was not to be put off, insisting that I took not two, but three ten pound notes, and maintaining that until he had left the field to assist Doreen to turn the wayward hounds, he had been more than satisfied with The Comet. In fact, the horse had given him the best ride he had ever had.

We were all deeply impressed by this show of open-handed sportsmanship. Lady Jennifer, in particular, was quite overcome and fussed over

Mr McLoughlin, offering him tea and brushing his jacket, and setting him on his way with promises of even better sport on the day of the opening meet. "And not a *mention* of payment," she warned him. "We shall be *delighted* to mount you, *absolutely* free of charge." Even I nodded agreement to this, secure in the knowledge that Mr McLoughlin's sense of fair play would never allow it.

After Mr McLoughlin had departed, and to my utter amazement, not only did my father stay for tea and sit on the sofa nibbling an iced fancy of a particular poisonous shade of green, but he and Lady Jennifer got on like a house on fire. The expected interrogations regarding wages and other matters related to gainful employment failed to occur and in no time at all they were both sitting on the sofa, sipping gin of dubious origin and giggling in a remarkably silly manner, whilst my father's jacket steamed in front of the electric fire. My father was still in a good humour when he drove away an hour or so later, seated on a split *Equivite* bag for the better protection of his person. He had invited Lady Jennifer to lunch the following week.

In due course Nigella and Henrietta returned, still boiling with excitement over the fabulous sport they had seen and totally unaware that anything untoward had happened to their client. When I related all that had taken place, Henrietta was vastly amused, but Nigella got into rather a state, maintaining that it was her fault for failing to watch The Comet who invariably took off when his head was turned for home. She was appalled to hear of Mr McLoughlin's injury and of the desecration of the Morris Minor and even the sight of the three ten pound notes failed to banish her remorse.

By the time we had finished in the stables, Nigella had worked herself up into a fever of anguish which Henrietta said was quite a regular occurrence due to over excitement after hunting, being a question of genetics and an inherited trait which had occasioned some of the Fane ancestors to have completely lost their marbles. This was hardly a comfort to Nigella who, far from being her calm and careful self, went around the yard as if demented, spilling the corn and dressing the horses in the wrong rugs, with her eyes unnaturally bright and two red spots burning on her cheeks.

When we finally repaired to the kitchen there was a letter waiting for us on the table. It was from Thunder and Lightning Limited, and it informed us that we could expect the three hunters to arrive two days prior to the opening meet. They had noted our terms with pleasure and found them to be extremely reasonable.

All this was too much for Nigella who, when Henrietta had read the letter aloud, placed her head on the kitchen table and sobbed and sobbed.

I felt a bit weak at the knees myself.

Two days later, we were out exercising when we passed some horses in a dealer's field. There was nothing unusual in this as we passed the field practically every time we rode out. It was usually peopled with a few nondescript animals and a flock of geese who sometimes opened their wings and hissed at us, making the horses shy. Today the geese were on the far side of the field amongst some rank clumps of grass, and they didn't bother us, but amongst the plain and pottery dealer's stock, there was a magnificent bay horse.

"Heavens," Nigella exclaimed. "Just look at that in Harry Sabin's field!" And we stopped to have a look.

The horse was a threequarter-bred gelding of about sixteen-two and he was absolutely beautiful. He was a rich, dark, whole colour with black points, and when he trotted across the field to investigate our horses, he moved like a dream.

"He certainly is some horse," Henrietta said admiringly. "You don't see too many with his sort of quality."

"You don't see too many with his sort of quality in Harry Sabin's field," Nigella said. "I wonder how he came by it?" She leaned forward over the old bay mare's bony shoulder and tickled the bay gelding under its chin. "He's very friendly."

The bay gelding stretched out its neck enquiringly towards the old bay mare. He wasn't clipped, and his thick coat had a soft, satiny gloss. The old bay mare squealed and tossed her mane like a four-year-old.

"There has to be something wrong with it," Henrietta decided. "There has to be a snag somewhere; otherwise Harry Sabin wouldn't have it. He doesn't deal in high class animals like this." She stood up in her stirrups and peered over the hedge at the horse's lower limbs, as if she expected to discover some appalling deformity.

I stood in the lane with Nelson and the bad-tempered chestnut and I thought that the bay horse looked familiar. I had seen him somewhere before.

91

"It might not be something you can see," Nigella pointed out. "It could be gone in the wind or have an irregular heartbeat. It could be a crib-biter."

"It's the tall, thin man's horse," I told them. "The one Henrietta was going to offer him fifty pounds for."

We all stared at the bay horse.

"So it is," Nigella said, astonished.

"Let's go and ask Harry Sabin how much he wants for it," Henrietta said. "It might be cheap."

We rode down a track which led into a dirt yard. There were a few ramshackle buildings and a scruffy cottage with its thatch patched with corrugated iron. There were some chickens scratching in the dirt and a blue-eyed, cream pony was wandering loose, like a dog. A wiry, weathered little man in a brown warehouse coat was tinkering about under the bonnet of a cattle waggon.

"Harry!" Nigella called. "How much is the bay gelding?"

Harry Sabin looked up from his tinkering in a leisurely sort of manner. "Now, Miss Fane, which bay gelding would you be talking about?" he enquired.

"You know which one we mean, Harry," Henrietta said. "The one in the top field."

"Ah," Harry Sabin said in an enlightened tone. "*That* bay gelding."

"How much is it?" Nigella said.

Harry Sabin straightened up slowly and put down his spanner. "That bay gelding," he said ruminatively, "come very expensive."

"Come off it, Harry," Henrietta said impatiently. "How expensive?" The black horse, who was being led beside The Comet, began to dig a hole in the dirt with one of his front hooves. Henrietta jerked his headcollar rope and he stopped for a few seconds and then began again with the other foot.

"Why would you be interested in the bay gelding, Miss Fane?" Harry Sabin asked, narrowing his foxy eyes and squinting up at Henrietta. "Is it that you haven't enough mouths to feed already?"

"All right," Henrietta said, annoyed. "If that's how you feel. I wasn't going to buy it anyway." She turned The Comet towards the lane.

"Harry," Nigella pleaded. "Just give us a price; a rough idea of what he's worth."

The blue-eyed, cream pony ambled round the back of the bad-tempered chestnut, who shuffled his quarters round, hoping to get a shot at it. I felt a bit impatient with the Fanes. They couldn't afford to buy the bay gelding. They were just wasting Harry Sabin's time, and he knew it. He softened though, as people often did, for Nigella.

"Well now," he said thoughtfully. "What he's worth, and what I'm asking for him, that's two entirely different things."

"Cut the cackle, Harry," Henrietta snapped. "How much?"

"Two thousand," Harry Sabin said.

"Heavens!" Nigella gasped. "*How* much?"

Harry Sabin shrugged his shoulders indifferently. "That's a class horse, that is."

"It jolly well needs to be for that sort of money," Henrietta snorted. "It's ridiculous. You'll never get it."

"Not from the likes of you, maybe," Harry Sabin said disparagingly. "He's entered for Warners

93

Wednesday week. They know a good horse when they see it in Leicestershire. They pay a good price there for a horse with class."

"It looks as if he could be the genuine article then," Henrietta said with regret as we rode back down the track. "It's a pity. Just imagine, he could have been ours if he'd been a wind-sucker or something."

The bay gelding trotted alongside us, displaying natural carriage and a long, low lingering stride behind two drooping strands of barbed wire. Without the tall, thin man on the top, he looked even more impressive. I took in his substance and his clean hard joints, his fine sloping shoulder and his beautifully balanced neck, his youth and his presence, and I wished with all my heart that I had two thousand pounds. If I had scoured the world for my ideal event horse, I might never have found him, and yet here he was in Harry Sabin's field. So close, and yet so impossibly out of reach.

9

A Tricky Customer

I just couldn't stop thinking about Harry Sabin's bay gelding. The same afternoon, perched on a wobbly saddle-horse, slapping whitewash on the ceiling of a stable allocated to the Thunder and Lighтning liveries, I decided that I would have to go back and have another look at him. I knew that if I could find one thing wrong with him, one defect which would make him unsuitable for eventing, I would be able to forget all about him and that would be the end of it.

I could hardly tell the Fanes where I was going because they would have thought I was mad, so I said that the smell of the paint was making me feel peculiar, and I put a saddle on Doreen's pony on the pretext of testing its wind to see if it would be fit for the opening meet. I trotted out of the yard feeling rather silly on the pony: it was only thirteen-two, and very narrow; my feet were almost level with its knees.

The bay gelding was no longer in the top field. The geese were there, running up to the hedge and making a brave show, and the dealer's stock were there, hardly troubling to raise their heads from the scrubby grass, but the bay gelding was not. There was nothing for it but to ride down the track into the dirt yard where Harry Sabin was still tinkering about under the bonnet of the waggon.

"Harry," I said. "Can I have a ride on the bay gelding?"

Harry Sabin straightened up and looked at me with his foxy eyes. "Now then, young lady," he said, "which bay gelding is that?"

I pointed to the bay gelding who was standing in one of the ramshackle buildings behind a slip rail.

"Well now," Harry Sabin said doubtfully. "That's a very expensive horse, that is."

"I'm looking for a good quality animal," I said. "I need a high class horse. I want to event." I was quite surprised to hear myself say it.

"Eventing is it?" Harry Sabin looked at Doreen's pony and scratched his head with the spanner. "That do seem a bit small for the job, I can see that."

"The pony isn't mine," I said hastily. "It's at livery with the Fanes. I came with them this morning. I work for them."

Mentioning the Fanes was obviously the wrong thing to do. Harry Sabin went back to his tinkering under the bonnet of the cattle waggon. "That isn't a horse for the Fanes," he said. "They don't pay that sort of price. I've sold a few horses to the Fanes in my time; they don't pay at all if they can help. I know the Fanes."

"It isn't for the Fanes I'm looking," I said. "It's for myself."

But Harry Sabin had lost interest in me as a potential customer. He didn't bother to reply. I got off the pony and tied him up with a piece of baler twine I found lying in the dirt. I leaned over the bonnet and faced Harry Sabin eyeball to eyeball. "Harry," I said. "The horse is the right type and he's the right height. He's also the right age, if he's the five-year-old I take him to be. But I have to be sure he has the scope and the temperament and the courage for the job. If you won't let me ride him, how will I know?"

Harry Sabin grinned at me. His teeth were the colour of old piano keys. "I daresay you won't," he said. "And I daresay you won't have two thousand pounds, neither."

"If the horse isn't suitable," I pointed out, "I shan't need to have."

"That you won't," Harry Sabin rubbed his chin in a thoughtful manner. "And you say it's not for the Fanes?"

"They don't even know I'm here," I said. "I made an excuse to get away. I can't stay long, otherwise they'll come after me."

This worked like a charm. "Best put the pony round the back then," Harry Sabin decided. "If they see that from the lane, that might just give you away." He seemed pleased to be part of a conspiracy against the Fanes. He waved his spanner in the direction of one of the tumbledown buildings. "Saddle's in there. Bridle's there as well, but that might need taking up a strap or two to fit." He went back to his tinkering looking vaguely triumphant.

I led the pony round the back of the buildings and I went to get the tack. The saddle was an awful old thing with a bumpy serge lining, and the bridle had a driving bit. I carried them over to where the bay gelding was standing. My heart was jumping with excitement as I ducked under the rail, took a few paces aside, and stared at my dream horse.

Close to, he was every bit as good as he had

looked in the field. He had the class and the conformation of a show horse. His coat was rich and glossy, his eyes were large and clear and intelligent, he had a good top line, strong, short cannon bones with tendons like iron bands, big flat knees, short sloping pasterns and healthy open feet. He also had a perfectly formed five-year-old's mouth. Try as I might, I couldn't fault him, and as Nigella had noticed, he was very friendly, and didn't once offer to put his ears back when I picked up his back feet and lifted his tail.

When I tacked him up, he opened his mouth obligingly for the driving bit, and stood like a rock whilst I girthed up the lumpy saddle. It was all too good to be true. I led him out into the yard. Harry Sabin shuffled across in order to leg me into the saddle and lead me to a rusted metal gate which opened into a field. The bay gelding had a long, swinging walk.

"He even walks like a show horse," I said.

"That's just what he was," Harry Sabin said. "A show horse."

"Why *was*?" I asked.

Harry Sabin shrugged and dragged open the rusty gate. "Temperament," he said.

"What do you mean?" I said. I had seen the horse out cubbing and hadn't felt that he had looked anything more than upset by bad horsemanship, but suddenly, especially after Doreen's pony, I felt a long way from the ground. "What's wrong with his temperament?" I asked.

But Harry Sabin refused to be drawn. "Just you sit tight, young lady," he warned. "That's a very expensive horse, that is, and don't you loose him. He's entered for Warners Wednesday week."

I rode through the gate feeling less than confident. Harry Sabin dragged the gate shut and went back to his tinkering. The dealer's stock in the top field trotted up to a gap in the hedge which had been filled in with a rusty bedstead and regarded the bay gelding with interest.

I walked and trotted him in a few cautious circles, noting his natural balance and steady head carriage and the fluent regularity of his stride which augured well for dressage. He didn't feel like a rogue horse. He was responsive and well-mannered and cantered a perfect figure eight with a simple change, and galloped for a short burst displaying a long, low stride, and a willingness to pull up when asked. My confidence almost fully restored, I looked round for something to jump.

There was nothing in the field except a broken down chicken coop, so it had to be that. I cantered him slowly towards it and left him to his own devices to see how, and if, he would tackle it. It was essential to find a horse who really enjoyed jumping because I needed a willing partner. The bay gelding pricked his ears forward and looked neither to the left nor the right, lengthened his stride into the coop and took off heavenwards in the most enormous leap I had ever experienced.

He jumped so high that I flew upwards out of the hateful little saddle and crashed down again right on to the pommel. It was agonizing. The bay gelding, feeling me loosened in the saddle, cantered on for a few strides with his head tucked into his chest, then he put in one almighty buck that sent me hurtling over his shoulder. I hit the ground with a thump that knocked all the breath out of my body and the bay gelding cantered off, cleared the bedstead with a yard to spare, and joined the dealer's stock who, overcome by the excitement of it all, thundered round and round the field like a cavalry charge.

I sat on the ground for at least five minutes, too sore and winded and shaken to move. I had always hated falling off and I had never got used to it. Eventually I staggered to my feet and made for the bedstead. My eyes were watering and I could hardly walk but I wanted to catch the bay gelding before Harry Sabin discovered that I had loosened his expensive animal, entered for Warners Wednesday week. I was halfway between the coop and the bedstead when another terrible thing happened. There was a hammering along the lane and the Fanes came into view mounted on Brenda's cob and Nelson.

Almost without thinking, I ducked down and made for the cover of the hedge, hoping against hope that the Fanes wouldn't notice the bay gelding in amongst all the others. But the sound of skidding hooves on tarmac told me that they had seen him and Henrietta's voice carried clearly across the field.

"Look," she said. "He's got a saddle on. And a bridle. He must have thrown his rider or something. We'd better catch him."

Horrified, I peered through the hedge and watched them ride along the lane until they came to the track which led to Harry Sabin's yard. Then I saw Henrietta dismount. She ducked under the wire, walked up to the bay gelding and took him by the rein. She led him towards the yard and Nigella followed with the horses.

Totally defeated, I limped to the gate, wondering how on earth I was going to explain my behaviour to the Fanes. Henrietta had never trusted me from the start and I could imagine how triumphant she would be to discover my deception. I had reached the gate to the yard and was still out of their line of vision when I heard Harry Sabin's voice.

"That's very good of you, Miss Fane," he said in a deeply respectful voice. "That's very good of you indeed. I was just expecting my lad to come and give him a spot of exercise and he just managed to slip the rail and get out of the shed. I'm much obliged to you and that's a fact."

"If you're that obliged, perhaps you'll consider dropping the price you're asking for him then," Henrietta said as she remounted Nelson. "Say four hundred?"

"That just isn't possible, Miss Fane," Harry Sabin said regretfully. "That wouldn't be economical at all. That's a very high class animal and I wouldn't take a penny less than two thousand for it, and that's the truth."

"Oh well," Henrietta said ungraciously. "Please yourself."

"I don't suppose you've seen our groom, Harry?" Nigella enquired. "The one who came with us this morning? She took out one of our liveries, a chestnut pony."

"Well now," Harry Sabin said, considering it. "I might have seen her along the lane not more than half an hour ago."

"Might have?" Henrietta said. "What do you mean, might have?"

"I can't say that it was definitely her," Harry Sabin said. "I've been busy on the waggon and there get to be a lot of horses along the lane."

As Henrietta and Nigella trotted back down the track, I eased my way carefully through the gate. Harry Sabin was standing by the cattle waggon holding the bay gelding, cackling with delight at having scored against the Fanes.

"Thanks for not giving me away, Harry," I said. "I thought I was done for then. I hope the horse is all right."

"That's lucky for you he is," Harry Sabin chuckled. "I told you not to loose him."

"But you didn't tell me what a wicked buck he had in him," I protested. "I might have stayed on if you had warned me."

But Harry Sabin was unrepentant. "But then he might not have bucked you," he said. "And I should have been sorry I'd mentioned it." He led the bay gelding back to his ruined stable. "A good sharp clout or two'll soon teach him some manners, young lady. It don't do to let them get the upper hand. He'll find his master in Leicestershire, and no mistake."

I followed them into the stable and watched Harry Sabin drag off the lumpy saddle. "He's a beautiful ride," I said. "I don't think I have ever ridden a better horse; and he certainly can jump."

"But can you stay on him when he do?" Harry Sabin wondered. "That's not much good if you can't." He pulled the bridle over the horse's ears. The bay gelding dropped the driving bit, stuck out

102

his head and lifted his upper lip in a gesture of disgust.

"Two thousand pounds is a lot of money," I said. "For a horse with a buck like that." It wasn't. Even with my limited experience, I knew that he would make twice the price at Leicester Sales. I ran my fingers through the bay gelding's silky coat and he turned his head and nudged hopefully at my pockets. I found him an old boiled sweet, gone soft and furry. "I'll give you fifteen hundred for him," I said.

Harry Sabin shouldered the saddle and regarded me in a sceptical manner.

"Subject to vet," I added.

"Subject to you getting the money," he said.

"Subject to you accepting my offer, for a start," I said.

I followed Harry Sabin across the dirt yard to the shed where he kept his awful saddlery; then I followed him back to the cattle waggon where he picked up his spanner and started tinkering. I had reluctantly decided that the conversation had come to an end when he straightened up and poked the spanner into my chest.

"You send your vet," he said. "And you bring me fifteen hundred in cash; I don't take no cheques since I've had a bad one off the Fanes. I'll keep the horse no more than a week. If you're not here with the cash by Monday week, he's off to Warners Wednesday, and that's the finish of it."

10

Can't Make It Tonight

Halfway back to the hall I had to dismount and walk beside the pony because I was so sore. I was within sight of the gates when a van slowed down alongside me. It was the flesh waggon from the kennels with Forster at the wheel.

"What happened to you?" he enquired, leaning over the passenger seat. "Did the brute throw you?"

"No," I said, embarrassed. "I'm walking because I'm too heavy for him. I'm giving him a rest."

"You're a liar," Forster said, grinning.

"I'm not," I said, but without conviction, because even if I wasn't yet, I supposed that I soon would be.

"I suppose you've fallen off Harry Sabin's bay gelding," Forster said.

I stopped walking and stared at him. Doreen's pony immediately dropped its head and started to graze.

Forster shrugged. "It was just a guess. Almost everyone has." He stopped the van and pulled up the handbrake.

"Including you?"

"Including William. The Master sent him to try it. He thought it might make a good hunt horse if he could get it at the right price."

"I'm glad he didn't," I said with relief. "It's far too good for a hunt horse."

"Thanks a lot," Forster said in a sarcastic tone. "I suppose you think we ill treat our horses, as well as our hounds."

"Not ill treat exactly," I said. "You're just too rough."

"We're paid to catch foxes," Forster said. "Not to practise the finer points of dressage." He leaned over further and pushed the passenger door open. "Sit down for a minute. You look as if you need to."

It crossed my mind that it might not be wise to sit in a van with Forster in a deserted lane, but I lowered myself carefully into the seat. There was a winch in the back of the van and a dead cow behind it. The cow was slimy and it stank. I averted my eyes hastily.

"Sorry," Forster said. "I've been to collect a casualty. I had to pull it out of the river."

"Nick," I said. "I'd be glad if you didn't say anything to anyone about me going to try the bay gelding. You're not supposed to know. No one is. It's supposed to be a secret."

"What on earth for?" he said curiously. "Don't tell me the Fanes are thinking of buying it."

"No," I said. "I am."

Now it was Forster's turn to stare. "You are?"

"I want it for an event horse," I said. "It's perfect. It's just the kind of horse I need."

"It's expensive though," Forster said. "At least," he corrected himself, "it's expensive for Harry Sabin."

"It's expensive for me as well," I admitted ruefully. "I'm broke. And I've got to find fifteen hundred pounds in cash by Monday week, otherwise it's going to Warners."

"How the devil are you going to do that?" Forster said, astonished.

"I haven't a clue," I said.

Forster laughed. Then, seeing that I wasn't laughing as well, he leaned his elbows on the driving wheel and rubbed his chin. "How about your parents?" he suggested.

"My father doesn't have any money to speak of," I said. "And what he has is invested in a building society. He wouldn't touch that, and anyway, he doesn't like horses."

We sat in silence for a few seconds.

"The only thing you can do," Forster said eventually, "is to find yourself a sponsor."

"I had thought of that," I said. "But who?"

"Well," Forster said, considering it. "It isn't as if you're a well known event rider with a string of past successes to your credit. You're an unknown quantity, so you can't expect the big companies to be interested. They wouldn't be prepared to back a struggling amateur because they are only in it for advertising purposes, and they wouldn't get enough publicity out of you to make it worth their while."

"I know," I said. "So it's hopeless really; and I can't go to my employers. The Fanes haven't a bean."

"The only person I can think of," Forster said, "is Felix Hissey."

"No thank you," I said flatly. "I don't think that would do at all."

"Why on earth not?" Forster wanted to know. "Felix Hissey is very into eventing and he might just be interested. His company sponsors two of the biggest events in the country."

"He also has an unexpected vacancy for a groom," I said. "Which you may well have a guilty conscience about."

"I see," Forster said resentfully. "So you've been tipped off by the scandalmongering Fanes."

"They aren't really scandalmongering," I protested. "They were only telling me for my own protection."

"I'd like to hear what else they told you," Forster said vengefully. "The next time I see those two, I'll crack their stupid heads together."

"You must admit though," I said, "that when you offered me the Hissey job, you did have an ulterior motive."

"So what if I had?" he said angrily. "It would have done you a good turn at the same time. Nobody in their right mind would want to work for the Fanes."

"Thanks for the compliment," I said. "Thanks a *lot*." Now it was my turn to feel nettled. I was fed up with Forster and the stench of the cow was beginning to turn my stomach. "I have to go now," I said. "I'm late already and the Fanes will be frantic."

"Oh no, Elaine," Forster said. "You're not going anywhere yet." He put out a hand and pinned me back in my seat.

I wasn't sure that I liked the way things were going. I had let go of the reins and Doreen's pony had moved further along the verge, still pulling at the grass. "I do have to go," I said anxiously. "The Fanes . . ."

"The Fanes can go to hell," Forster said. He put his arm round my shoulders.

I could see that I would have to make a firm stand if I was to keep the situation under control. I removed his arm. "I'm sorry, Nick," I said. "I really can't stay any longer. I am supposed to be working, after all, and there's a lot to be done in the yard; we've three new liveries coming in tomorrow."

Forster looked as if he might object, then he shrugged. "All right," he said. "If you're so determined to be conscientious, I'll see you on your day off. When is it?"

"Er . . . I haven't actually got one organized yet," I admitted. "We've been so busy, it didn't seem fair to ask."

"I don't suppose you've organized yourself any wages yet, either," he said in an exasperated tone.

"Well, no," I said. "How could I? There hasn't been any money coming into the yard. The Fanes are on their uppers. There didn't seem any point in going on about it."

"Honestly, Elaine," he exploded. "I said you were barmy the first time I saw you and I was right. You're the biggest idiot I've ever met! *Nobody* works without being paid for it; you must be round the twist!"

This was the last straw. I gave him a shove and dived for the door handle. "I'm not staying here to be shouted at," I told him. "I've had enough."

"Suit yourself," he said coldly. "Girls like you deserve all they get." He turned the key in the ignition. The engine roared.

"I *beg* your pardon?" I exclaimed. I felt my face flush with anger. "I think you might be mistaken there; *you're* the one with the lousy reputation!"

"I'm not talking about reputations," he said. "I'm talking about working for peanuts. I like my job; I like the hounds and the horses and the hunting, I

108

even like the foxes; but I wouldn't work for nothing, and my employers respect me enough to pay me a decent wage. You girl grooms moan about being underpaid and overworked, but it's your own fault, you let yourselves be exploited all the way along the line. You're fools." He kept his eyes on the road. "And you're one of the biggest fools of all, Elaine, if only you would realize it."

"I want to work with horses," I said indignantly. "I want a chance to event. I didn't realize that eventing yards were so few and far between, or that it was going to be so hard to find a job with a decent wage. People don't seem to be able to pay very much. There doesn't seem to be much money about in the horse world, when you get close enough to find out."

"Rubbish," Forster said, but his voice was suddenly less angry. "There is money in the horse world, but people have got used to having horse-mad girls on tap for cheap labour. It's going to take them a long time to learn that if they want a decent groom they have to pay a decent wage, even if it means they have to keep fewer horses."

I was touched by this, and even a little ashamed. "I'll talk to the Fanes," I decided. "Now that we've got these new liveries, I'll tackle them about my wages, and about my days off. Perhaps I am a fool, but you must admit that the Fanes are an extreme case; I can't help feeling sorry for them. They were once a very fine family, but they have fallen on such hard times; they are a dying breed."

"The Fanes," Forster said, "are a pain in the arse." He grinned. His humour was almost fully restored. "Elaine, if you really want to tackle Felix

Hissey about Harry Sabin's bay gelding, he'll be at the opening meet. He always parks his box in this lane; you can't miss it, it's a navy blue Lambourne. He leaves at two o'clock sharp every hunting day, and he comes back to his box for a quiet sandwich and a drink before he drives home. It might be a good opportunity to catch him. I can't promise that he'll be interested, but it's worth a try."

I was so delighted with this piece of information that I forgot about my injury, and the slimy cow, and Doreen's pony, who was almost at the Hall gates, having eaten himself home. I leaned over and gave Forster a peck on his cheek. This was a tactical error, because I somehow got caught up in his broody dark-fringed eyes and almost before I knew it, he had taken hold of the back of my neck and stretched out his other hand to turn off the ignition. He was just closing in when I saw two faces, framed in the window beyond his shoulder. It was the Fanes.

I let out an involuntary yelp. Forster drew back, startled, and turned round in his seat. When he saw the Fanes he wrenched open the door.

"What the hell are you up to?" he shouted in a furious voice. "Creeping about and spying on people!"

"We weren't actually creeping about," Nigella objected. "You didn't hear us coming. You had your engine running."

"How dare you play fast and loose with our groom anyway," Henrietta cried, her cheeks flushed with anger and excitement. "We guessed she was up to something! She said she was only going out to test the pony's wind and she's been gone for hours, she was going to meet you all the time!"

Forster jumped out of the van. "And what if she was?" he demanded angrily. "Since when have you been her nursemaid?"

I staggered out of the flesh waggon in order to cope with all this. My back had stiffened up and I was none too steady on my feet. I knew that I looked hot and dishevelled, and in the circumstances, I could hardly blame the Fanes for jumping to conclusions.

"Oh, Elaine," Nigella said reproachfully. "How *could* you?"

"And with *him*, of *all* people," Henrietta shouted. "After we warned you about his reputation!"

Forster took a threatening step towards Henrietta.

"Don't you dare lay a finger on me!" she shrilled. "I know your type!"

"Not, perhaps, quite as well as you would like," Forster said in an icy voice.

Henrietta backed away, her face crimson. "How dare you," she choked.

"We honestly didn't mean to spy on you, Elaine," Nigella said in a harassed tone. "But you had been gone for ages, and you had said you felt peculiar. We were getting anxious and then we saw the pony loose on the grass verge; we *are* supposed to be responsible for you, whilst you are living under our roof."

"Or to be strictly accurate," Forster snarled, "half of one." He jumped into the flesh waggon, slammed the door, and roared off down the lane.

I walked painfully up the drive behind the Fanes, leading the pony, whose mouth dripped green froth. My head was spinning. Suddenly there were so many things to consider that I didn't know where to start.

Certainly I couldn't deny that I had spent the afternoon with Forster without revealing the truth or
telling lies, so I decided that the best thing to do was
to leave things as they were and let the Fanes think
what they liked. But for the rest of the afternoon,
you could have cut the atmosphere in the stable yard
with a knife.

I got through evening stables early and went back to
the Hall to telephone the vet. He agreed to examine
the bay gelding the following day and I arranged to
ring him at his surgery in the evening for his report.
After that I boiled some kettles of water to augment
my bath and soaked my aches and pains and washed
my hair. Then I went down to the kitchen prepared
to do some cooking because by this time I was
feeling pretty remorseful about upsetting the Fanes.

I found the kitchen table heaped with offerings for
a Help The Aged jumble sale, currently being organized by Lady Jennifer, who obligingly cleared a
corner for me whilst I stirred the Aga into action.
Amongst the pressed sugar bowls and the fairground
Alsatians, there was a portable television set.

"It can't *possibly* be a working model," Lady
Jennifer decided. "It would be just *too* generous for
words."

"It won't be much use to anyone if it doesn't
work," I pointed out. "You will have to test it."

"Could you be an absolute *angel* and test it for
me, Elaine?" she wondered, considering a wobbly
plastic cakestand before applying a fifteen pence
sticker to it. "I simply haven't a *clue* about
electricity."

I promised to try it later. When Lady Jennifer had

priced all the junk, she swept it into cardboard boxes and transported it to the front hall where jumble stretched from floor to ceiling, emanating a smell of B.O. and mothballs. A few minutes later she raced through the kitchen in her crumpled raincoat, bound for a spell of night duty with the Samaritans.

"Oh," Henrietta said when she came into the kitchen. "Biscuits."

"And a pie," I said. "And a cake and a pudding. It's a sort of apology for this afternoon."

"As a matter of fact," Nigella said. "We've been talking about that."

"And we've decided," Henrietta added with her mouth full of biscuit. "That we were probably a little hasty. After all, it's your life, and you're over the age of consent, so you can do what you like."

"Oh," I said, taken aback. "Thank you very much."

"Although we must point out," Nigella said, "that we are a little concerned about your choice of friends." She leaned over the table and sniffed the cake appreciatively.

"And as we have our reputation to consider," Henrietta went on, adopting a serious tone. "We must ask you to protect yourself against any possible consequences."

"I see," I said. I wondered what possible consequences could arise from a peck on the cheek.

"I hope you don't mind us being so forthright," Nigella said. "But Nick Forster does have a very sticky reputation, although one has to admit that he is rather devastating to look at."

"If you happen to like the dark, dangerous type,"

113

Henrietta said, licking her unwashed fingers. "Personally, I don't. I think he's a nasty piece of work. By the way," she added, "where did the television come from?"

"It's a jumble offering," I said. "I promised that we would test it."

Henrietta kicked off her wellingtons and transferred her attention from the biscuits to the television set. There was no aerial, so she spent some time poking bits of wire into the back and fiddling with the controls, achieving a lot of zizzing noise and a row of shivering dots on the screen. Finally she had the brilliant idea of wiring the set up to the lightning conductor. This was a wild success and resulted in an excellent picture.

As the Fanes had never previously owned a television, the jumble set was an event worthy of celebration. Nigella disappeared into the depths of the cellar and returned decorated with cobwebs, clutching a dirt encrusted bottle of cloudy red wine out of which she strained terrifying lumps through a tea cloth. Then we sat round the kitchen table eating pie and taking cautious sips of the wine, with our eyes glued to the television set, and it was all very jolly.

By the time we had started our second glass of wine, we were even jollier still. The Fanes were anticipating their high class liveries due to arrive the next morning, and I was imagining myself collecting fifteen hundred pounds from Felix Hissey and riding into the yard in triumph on Harry Sabin's bay gelding. We were watching a top twenty record show.

"Look at him," Henrietta said, waving her fork at the screen. "He's got striped hair."

114

The singer with striped hair was replaced by the compère who had two lots of earrings and a furry chest.

"We've got a real treat for you now, folks," he crowed. "Live in the studio; currently number eight in the charts and climbing fast – *Can't Make it Tonight*, by Thunder and Ligh⚡ning Limited!"

Nigella laid down her fork on the table. "What did he say?" she said.

As the first beats of *Can't Make it Tonight* thundered out, the group appeared on the screen. There were three of them. They wore black leotards and leg-warmers which revealed unexpected areas of puny, unattractive flesh. They wore necklaces, bangles and earrings, vivid lipstick and heavy eye makeup. They didn't have striped hair. They didn't have any hair at all. They were completely bald.

There was no mistake, because as the camera followed their gyrations across the stage, it caught the name of the group emblazoned across the front of the drums. Thunder and Ligh⚡ning Limited it said, with the familiar jag of lightning replacing the t.

11

High Class Liveries

The next morning we set about morning stables in an agony of apprehension, listening with half an ear for the sound of the horsebox which would deliver our three liveries. We didn't know what to expect. We didn't dare to imagine. But as the day passed and no horsebox arrived, our expectations began to fade.

By five o'clock it was already dark, and as we lit the barn lanterns which hung outside every other stable door, creating our own Dickensian world of flickering golden light and stamping hooves, an atmosphere of ostlers and old inns and stagecoaches, we began to realize that our liveries were not going to materialize. The general feeling was of anticlimax, coupled with a mixture of relief and dismay.

Henrietta slammed the doors of the prepared stables in a gesture of disgust. "They were never coming in the first place," she said. "It was probably a trick. It was just a stupid joke." She gave me a suspicious look, as if I might be responsible for it.

"Perhaps it's just as well," Nigella decided. "They weren't exactly the type of clients we were hoping for. They might have worn lipstick at the opening meet. They might have worn mascara and eye shadow and spangles on their cheeks."

"And just think of those three bald heads," I said. "Even with a velvet cap on top, they would still have

116

looked a sight." Now that it wasn't going to happen, we could voice our unspoken, unspeakable fears.

"They probably have a drink problem," Nigella said. "And they might have had groupies. There might have been unmentionable goings-on in the back of the horsebox."

"Not only that," I said. "But I expect they are on drugs. They probably smoke pot or worse. They might have arrived at the opening meet stoned out of their minds. They would have got us thrown out of the Hunt."

"All the same," Henrietta grumbled. "We could have used their seventy-five pounds a week."

Nigella and I fell silent, depressed by the thought of the money aspect; and in the silence we heard the unmistakable hum of an engine on the drive.

The custom-built horsebox turned into the yard under the clock arch. The stable lanterns were mirrored in its gleaming black coachwork. They caught at the Rolls Royce insignia on the bonnet. When the driver jumped out, the door with its narrow red trim closed behind him with a discreet clunk. Muffled scraping noises issued from the rear of the box.

"Are you the Misses Fane?" the driver asked. He wasn't wearing lipstick. He wasn't bald. He was a thin, blond-haired, anxious looking man in a tweed jacket and Newmarket boots.

The Fanes stared at the horsebox with their mouths open. I said that we were. I asked, although I already knew, if he had brought the horses for Thunder and Ligh?ning Limited.

The driver introduced himself as Chick Hayes. He handed me a set of keys. Special delivery, he said, of three horses and a horsebox. "The Lads" had suggested that he should leave us to it. They had a gig tonight in Norwich and he was supposed to be in charge of the lighting. So we would have to excuse him if he nipped off because he was already late. And "The Lads" didn't like him to be late; they didn't like it at all.

I asked Chick Hayes if we could expect "The Lads" to be attending the opening meet. To my relief he said no. They had a concert on Saturday and they wouldn't be hunting until Thursday, when we should arrange to have the horses plaited and loaded for ten fifteen sharp. As the horses were all new, he said, it might be a good idea if we gave them an hour or two with the hunt on Tuesday, so that we could give "The Lads" an idea of what they were like to handle. Then, if any of them turned out to be tricky, we could ring him up to enable him to swop it for a better one. He couldn't chance anything happening to one of "The Lads", they were a valuable commodity. And the Insurance Company didn't like the idea of "The Lads" going hunting; they didn't like it at all.

Even the Fanes were taken aback by the revelation that "The Lads" hadn't felt it was necessary to select their own hunters; and that any bad ones would be exchanged as if they were no more than a pound of apples. I felt that such a cavalier attitude could spell trouble in store, and I was rendered even more uneasy when I remembered that "The Lads" had not felt it necessary to send anyone to inspect our yard before they had accepted our livery terms. I was heartily glad that we were to be spared the presence of Thunder and Lightning Limited at the opening meet.

When Chick Hayes had sped off towards the Norwich gig in a Bedford van which had come along behind, the beautiful horsebox was left in solitary splendour in the centre of the yard. The lanterns reflected in the paintwork like orange globes and the Fanes and I stood and stared at it, mesmerized, like children round a Christmas tree.

"Well," I said eventually. "I suppose we had better get the horses out."

I began to unbolt the ramp. The Fanes, after a moment's hesitation, came to help. The ramp swung down smoothly to reveal three horses, a bay, a chestnut and a blue roan, staring at us over partitions padded with real hide. I had seen luxury horseboxes before, but even the box which Hans Gelderhol used to transport his event horses had been nothing like this. The paintwork was sparkling, unblemished white, the padding was soft black leather, the floors were fitted with anti-slip matting, and the inside of the box was lit like a film set.

Nigella unbolted the breast bar and untied the bay, who stepped down the ramp in an unhurried, mannerly way, pausing at the foot to look round at his new surroundings. He was a quality blood horse with a sensible, kind expression. He wore a black mohair rug piped in red with a jag of lightning in the corner instead of initials. He had matching kneecaps and tailguard, red bandages and a nut brown anticast roller and headcollar with solid brass fittings.

"Wow," Henrietta breathed, taking it all in. "Wow."

"Now this really *is* my idea of a high class livery,"

Nigella said, delighted. "If we can attract clients with horses like these, we are made. Our problems are over."

"From what I have seen and heard of 'The Lads'," I reminded them, "our problems might only just be beginning."

We stabled the horses and changed their mohair rugs for lined and piped jute night rugs with pure new wool under-blankets. Then we fed them and began to unload the saddlery from the groom's compartment in the horsebox. It was all top quality German workmanship with stainless steel bits, stirrup irons and buckles. In the homely light of a lantern suspended from the centre beam, we stowed the fine saddlery in our shabby tackroom and folded the beautiful rugs carefully on the centre table. When it was all finished we stood back and drank it all in; the silvery gleam of the metalwork, the soft glow of fine supple leather, the luxury of the rugs with their scarlet piping, the glitter of the brass fitted headcollars.

"One day," Henrietta said, "all our saddlery will be like this." And her eyes were hungry in the lantern light.

Nigella said nothing, and I knew that she was thinking what I was thinking. That if it didn't work out; if it turned out to be wrong and all this richness was taken away again, how terribly hard it would be to bear. That after all our struggles, after all the moth-eaten rugs, the patched and threadbare blankets, the old and withered leather, the rusted and pitted metalwork, to be able to feast our eyes on such fabulously extravagant things was food for the soul. So we stood looking but not saying, for a long time, whilst the stable cat purred around our ankles.

After all that, I almost forgot to ring the vet. I left the Fanes investigating the baby cooker and the fridge and the buttoned hide seating in the living compartment of the horsebox, and fled up to the Hall to get the report on Harry Sabin's bay gelding.

I was only just in time because the vet had finished his surgery and was in the act of going out of the door in his hat and coat when the telephone rang. He was pleased to inform me that the bay gelding had a completely clean bill of health which would cost me fifteen pounds. Yes, he was sound in every way and as far as he could tell, eminently suitable for a tough competitive sport such as eventing. There was just one thing that he felt bound to mention. That when he had been galloped to test his wind, and to assess how quickly his heartbeat and respiration returned to normal after exertion, he had put in a buck, the violence of which had almost launched Harry Sabin's lad into outer space.

12

Flight of The Comet

On the morning of the opening meet the Fanes appeared in beautifully cut, navy blue habits with scarlet waistcoats. Their wild hair was wild no longer, it was coiled and netted below silk hats. They wore veils over their faces. They looked absolutely beautiful. I stared at them in amazement, quite unable to speak.

"We thought you would like it," Nigella said. "We did it as a surprise. We don't actually have any proper hunt coats and breeches and things. The habits belong to Mummy. They are almost antique."

"We have to live up to our high class image, after all," Henrietta said. "Although if we break our necks, it will probably be your fault. We haven't ridden sideways for ages."

They tripped off across the cobbles to heave down the side-saddles which reposed under canvas covers on the topmost brackets of the tack room, leaving me to organize the rest of our party.

There were seven horses going from the yard. Mr McLoughlin, not surprisingly, had expressed a desire not to be reunited with The Comet. Nigella determined to ride him herself, which allowed him the use of the mare-who-sometimes-slipped-a-stifle. Henrietta was taking the black horse, Brenda was taking her pink-nosed cob, Doreen was taking her pony, and a friend of hers was hiring the bad-tempered chestnut. This had left me with the scintillating choice between the old bay mare and Nelson.

I was a bit worried about the old bay mare because when I had ridden her out to exercise a few days previously, I had thought she was off-colour. The Fanes had dismissed this as a figment of my imagination, especially in view of the fact that I had taken her temperature which had been completely normal, 100.5 after two minutes. But since then I had noticed that she hadn't been finishing up her feeds, and although I couldn't find anything specific to put my finger on, I was uneasy about taking her hunting. So it had to be Nelson.

Taking Nelson actually suited my plans perfectly. The fact that he wasn't hunting fit and was only up to half a day provided me with an excuse to leave early. I planned to take him slowly, keeping to the rear of the field, so that I could slip away undetected at one o'clock and be waiting for Felix Hissey when he returned to his box at two.

We set off down the drive in a little cavalcade led by Brenda's cob, slapping down his soup-plate feet in a purposeful manner, his persil-white tail swinging above his thickset hocks.

"We're going to be late, Busy Bee," Brenda grumbled. "It'll take half an hour to get there and all the free booze will have gone."

But the Fanes were unconcerned about being late and we progressed at a leisurely pace. The lanes were jammed with horseboxes and trailers and I felt my heart speed up under my hunting shirt as we passed the navy blue Lambourne not far from the

Hall gates. We were overtaken by throngs of late-comers hammering along towards the meet. Children cantered past us along the grass verges with their ponies already in a lather, and now and again we drew aside for a solitary scarlet-coated sub-scriber, loping along at a ground-covering trot, striking sparks from the lane.

The opening meet, traditionally held on the first day of November, is an important social event in the hunt calendar and I was anxious that we should create a good impression. I was satisfied that the horses looked as good as was possible in the short time that had been available. We had all worked hard on them and the Fanes, after a characteristic objection to plaiting up ("We never plait manes," Nigella said. "We find it a waste of time,") relented after they had watched me plait Doreen's pony. Henrietta, who had never hitherto plaited anything other than her own tangle of hair, proved a dab hand, moving from stable to stable with her damp sponge and comb, needles and thread, plaiting up the horses with incredible speed and neatness, singing in her clear, high voice, a plaiting song composed on the spot.

> "Silver needles and golden manes,
> Cold in the stable, ice on the lanes,
> Silver needles and golden manes,
> Seven hunt plaits for the Galloping Fanes."

When we got to the village green where the meet was taking place, it was murder. Brenda and Doreen battled their way through the crowds towards the pub carpark where the tail end of the punch was being distributed.

The rest of us waited well away from the scrum, in the centre of which I caught the occasional glimpse of Forster in his blue velvet cap, his dark hair curling over the collar of his scarlet coat; he looked out of temper; and William, hot and flustered with the effort of keeping hounds together, had a face the colour of a radish.

I looked around at the scarlet-coated subscribers, wondering which of them was Felix Hissey. I hadn't the remotest idea what he looked like. There must have been five or six hundred mounted followers at the meet, not to mention all the foot people. I couldn't imagine how we were going to get any hunting at all, but Nigella said that the Huntsman would draw all the worst coverts first, in the hope that those members of the field who had only come out to be seen and photographed would become discouraged and go home.

The Galloping Fanes in their stunning outfits attracted a lot of attention at the meet. They smiled obligingly for the photographers who seemed to be under the impression that they were visitors from the Quorn. They certainly looked very grand, but I was a little worried about how Nigella would fare on The Comet without a leg on each side.

Nigella's prediction came true in that we had drawn three coverts before we got a run, by which time the field had thinned to about two hundred. This was still bad enough because there was a melée in every gateway and a queue of adamant refusers at every jumpable place. To get any sort of ride at all I had to take my own line. This seemed a good idea until I got my first taste of Nelson's jumping system.

Nelson's missing eye made no difference to him on the flat whatsoever but his method of tackling an obstacle was unconventional to say the least. He galloped towards it with great enthusiasm, holding his head low and cocked slightly to one side, giving the impression of rushing through space with nothing in front. But as he neared the obstacle he gradually began to slow up, until by the time he had reached it he was almost at a standstill. Then suddenly, just as I had decided that he had refused, he sprang over it like a cat and took off at the speed of light towards the next ditch.

This, together with the fact that I was still sore from my collision with the bay gelding and unable to concentrate on hunting due to my forthcoming meeting with Felix Hissey, didn't add up to a very enjoyable morning, and it was with a feeling of relief that I looked at my watch and saw that it was after one o'clock, time to leave.

Hounds were in the vicinity of home as Nelson and I traversed the lanes. Groups of people were already engaged in loading up their horses, or leaning against their cars and horseboxes, smoking or gossiping or eating sandwiches. With Nelson's stitched up eye socket and his bobbing ears in front of me, and the hollow clop of his boxy feet below me, I practised what I would say when I met Felix Hissey, and the more I practised, the more nervous I felt. I knew I had to convince him that the bay gelding and I had a great future, that we were a solid investment, but when it came to finding the right words it was not so easy. Whichever way I put it, I was still asking him to part with fifteen hundred pounds, probably more, which was pretty bare-faced cheek. I could hardly blame him if he saw me off with a flea in my ear, but I should have to risk that. I wanted the bay gelding more than I had ever wanted anything, and Felix Hissey was my only hope. I had to try to talk him into it.

Nelson bounced over a heap of rust red bricks which was all that remained of the demesne wall and trotted over the spongy old turf. As I was on the far side of the park, I decided to ride along the river bank until I came to the bridge where the lane crossed the river and where, not more than five hundred yards away, I had seen the navy blue Lambourne horsebox parked earlier in the day. I was just consoling myself with the thought that at least my plans had not been jinxed by the Fanes, when I became aware of thundering hooves somewhere in the distance behind me.

I turned round in my saddle, half expecting to see the young entry with William or Forster at their heels. I saw The Comet instead. There was a steady relentlessness about his coming and as he came nearer, I saw that Nigella was shouting and hauling uselessly at the reins. She had completely lost control.

I pulled up Nelson, cursing the Fanes for their gift of turning up when they weren't wanted, thinking that now I had the additional worry of shaking off Nigella before I got to see Felix Hissey. I was sure that The Comet would stop when he got to us but The Comet did no such thing. He swept past without faltering in his stride with Nigella clinging on, her face taut with horror. It took me a few seconds to realize why. It was because the only thing that separated The Comet from his stable was the river.

I clapped my heels into Nelson's astonished sides and he leapt into a gallop. His neck stretched out and the clods flew but it was useless to try to catch The Comet. I could see the river looming closer by the second, but the sight of it did nothing to daunt the runaway. He galloped furiously and unwaveringly towards the bank and he launched himself into the air. I heard Nigella's terrified scream as they appeared to hang in space and the next moment there was a tremendous splash as they hit the water. They vanished from sight and their backwash flooded the banks.

As Nelson skidded on to the bank, I threw myself out of the saddle and stared helplessly into the river. I had no idea of what I should do. After a few seconds I saw The Comet's head emerge a little way down stream, but Nigella didn't come up at all. I stripped off my jacket and struggled to free myself from my boots. Nelson, quite oblivious to the emergency, dropped his head and began to graze.

I was just about to jump into the water when I heard a faint noise from the opposite bank and first Nigella's arm and then her head appeared under a willow. At the same instant I saw Henrietta galloping towards us on the opposite bank, followed by Mr McLoughlin on the mare-who-sometimes-slipped-a-stifle. Screaming to them that Nigella was in the river, I jumped on to Nelson in my stockinged feet and made for the bridge.

When I arrived on the opposite bank, Nigella was being hauled to the water's edge on the thong of Mr McLoughlin's hunting whip. We leaned over and dragged her out of the river, and we sat her, heaving and choking and blue with cold, upon a stump. Water streamed from her beautiful habit and her hair was plastered to her shoulders.

"The Comet," she gasped as soon as she was able to speak. "He's drowned!"

"Never," cried Mr McLoughlin valiantly. He pointed to The Comet's bobbing head. The horse was swimming strongly away from us, straight up the middle of the river.

"Oh," Nigella cried. "The horrible brute." She burst into agonized sobs.

Henrietta and I set off after The Comet along the bank, hoping to tempt him out with the promise of equine company. But The Comet was having none of it. We followed him across the park, over the lane, and for almost a mile until the river had widened into mud flats fringed with reed. There, amongst rotting barges and watched by two majestic swans, The Comet hit the shallows and waded out, only slightly obstructed by the side-saddle, which had settled itself beneath his belly.

Henrietta led him home with his sides heaving like a bellows. His saddlery was stuck with reeds, and steam rose from his every part. Henrietta herself was not the elegant sight she had once been.

I followed on Nelson, trying to ignore the curious looks we collected from the occupants of land rovers and horseboxes returning from the hunt. I was grieved to know that I looked just as odd, hatless and bootless and jacketless, with a hole in the elbow of my yellow hunting shirt and the ends of my stock flying in the breeze.

"We shall have to sell The Comet after this,"

Henrietta said grimly. "He'll have to go. We can't possibly keep him any longer. He will kill someone in the end." And as a navy blue Lambourne horse-box inched past us in the lane and I hid my face to preclude any future recognition, she added, as one who is struck with an extremely sensible idea, "Perhaps we can send him to Warners with Harry Sabin's bay gelding."

13

A Raison d'Etre

All I could think about now was getting to see Felix Hissey. I knew that it was no earthly use waiting until the next hunting day because we had to take the Thunder and Lighɔning liveries out and I would never find an excuse to shake off the Fanes. So I watched and waited for my chance, and on Monday afternoon it came. A lorry trundled down the drive to collect the jumble.

After we had loaded the junk and tied a tarpaulin over it, the Fanes and Lady Jennifer squashed into the cab beside the driver to organize the unpacking at the village hall. Within five minutes of their departure, I was speeding along in the shooting brake, on my way to the pickle factory in Bury St Edmunds.

The pickle factory was in the old part of the town behind a Georgian terrace. Above the gates there was a wrought iron arch in the centre of which there was a sign in the shape of a round-faced, red-cheeked man with a jolly smile and a crown studded with silverskin onions and chilli peppers. I drove into the yard and was directed towards the office by a white-coated man unloading cauliflowers from a lorry.

The office was up a lot of narrow flights of stairs above the factory where lines of women in overalls, with their hair tied up in scarves, shouted to each other over the clank of the machinery and the clink of glass and the roar of piped music. There was a powerful smell of vinegar.

Behind a door at the top of the last flight of stairs I came upon the round-faced, red-cheeked man of the sign, bending over a desk, sniffing at little piles of orange powder.

"Take a sniff," he invited. "I'm trying to decide which has the best bouquet."

I was breathless from the climb, and in my anxiety to do the right thing, I leaned over and inhaled the nearest pile. The fine dust rose up into my nostrils. I sneezed, dispersing orange powder in a cloud all over the desk.

"No, no," the Pickle King said in reproof. "Not like that, like this. *Gently*." He leaned over another pile and gave a short, delicate sniff, closing his eyes and flaring his nostrils. "You test the aroma. You don't take it like snuff."

I tried again. "I can't smell anything at all," I confessed.

"That's because you haven't a nose," the Pickle King said with regret. "There are not many about these days. People don't realize what a disastrous effect our polluted environment has on the olfactory senses; a good nose today is a very rare find." He settled himself down behind the desk and waved me into a chair. "As you haven't a nose," he said cheerfully, "perhaps you should begin by telling me what other redeeming qualities you have." He beamed at me expectantly.

"I beg your pardon?" I said.

"Your qualifications," he said. "Your experience. Have you ever worked in a pickle factory before?"

"Mr Hissey," I said nervously. "I don't want a job in the factory."

A look of enlightenment spread over the Pickle King's cherubic face. "Then you must be the girl groom young Forster was telling me about," he said. "I should have guessed. I can see you are the outdoor type."

"I haven't actually come about the groom's job either," I said.

The Pickle King's face fell. He frowned.

"I've come about Harry Sabin's bay gelding," I said, and I blurted out the whole story; about my eventing ambitions and the misery of not being able to find a job which paid a living wage, and of having to accept work with the Fanes, and how we had come across the bay gelding in Harry Sabin's field and how, if I didn't do something about it, it was going to Warners on Wednesday week. I was just mentioning the importance of having the fifteen hundred in cash, when the Pickle King held up a restraining hand.

"Wait a minute," he said in a disbelieving voice. "Am I hearing you correctly? Are you asking *me* to buy *you* a horse?"

"Not exactly," I said, but then, "well, yes. I suppose I am."

"But I hardly know you," he exclaimed, and his eyes were round with astonishment. "We only met a few minutes ago!"

"I don't actually want you to buy the horse for *me*," I tried to explain. "I just want you to put up the money. It would actually belong to you. You would own it."

"Oh," the Pickle King said. "How extremely generous."

"I don't seem to have put this very well," I said anxiously. "But the truth of the matter is that I want to event and I've found the perfect horse, but I haven't any money. I need a sponsor."

"I don't sponsor people," the Pickle King said firmly.

"Not people," I said. "Only one person. Only me."

"Especially people I don't know," he added. "So I'll say good morning." He scrambled up from behind his desk and made for the door.

I grabbed him by his jacket. "Mr Hissey," I said desperately. "I only need a chance. I have a promising future; ask Hans Gelderhol."

The Pickle King paused with his hand on the door knob. "Hans Gelderhol?" he said. "*That* Hans Gelderhol?" He nodded towards a framed photograph on the wall.

"Oh yes," I said. "That's the one I mean."

"And Hans Gelderhol thinks you're good?"

"Ask him," I said. "Ring him up. Ring him now."

The Pickle King made his way back to the desk and stretched out a hand towards the telephone. He hesitated. "If Hans Gelderhol thinks you're so good," he enquired, "why doesn't he take you on himself?"

"He did ask me," I said. "I refused."

The Pickle King flopped back into his chair. "You refused a job with Hans Gelderhol?" he said incredulously. "You *refused*?"

I nodded.

"Why?"

"Personal reasons," I said.

The Pickle King looked at me suspiciously. "What personal reasons?" he asked.

"They're personal," I said indignantly.

The Pickle King waved me back into my chair. "I only asked," he said placatingly, "because most girls would give an arm and a leg to work for Hans Gelderhol."

"I know," I said. "Hans Gelderhol can have any girl he wants, and now and again they do get a ride. But they don't get paid good wages, and they don't get the good horses. He keeps those for himself."

"Well, naturally," the Pickle King said. "He *is* the star." He stared at me thoughtfully. "So you wouldn't join the bandwagon," he said. "You didn't fancy it, eh?"

"Didn't fancy what?" I said faintly.

The Pickle King chuckled. "Don't think I don't know the Golden Boy," he said. "I know Hans. I know him very well indeed."

"There was nothing improper," I said. "I was just a student. But the inference is that if you haven't a wealthy family behind you, you haven't a chance. I want to prove that it isn't necessarily so. I want to do it on my own."

"Correction," the Pickle King said. "You want to do it on my money."

I couldn't deny it.

The Pickle King frowned at me over the desk, and his forehead was furrowed with genuine perplexity. "Assume for one moment, Miss Would-Be-Event-Rider," he said, "that I rang Hans Gelderhol and he gave me a glowing report on your potential; then further assume that I purchased this bay gelding on

135

your behalf. What would I stand to gain from it? Can you give me one valid reason why I should back a completely untried novice horse and rider? Why I should spend fifteen hundred pounds on a total stranger?"

It was the question I had been dreading. There was nothing for it but to tell the truth. "You were the only person I could think of," I said. "Everyone knows you are interested in eventing, you must be, or you wouldn't be a patron. I know you sponsor events and give prize money and expensive trophies to those who have made it to the top; I thought there might be a chance that you would consider helping someone right at the bottom for a change." It sounded unlikely, even to my own ears.

"I might," the Pickle King said.

I could hardly believe it. I almost jumped out of my chair.

The Pickle King held up a restraining hand. "I only said that I might, not that I would." But his eyes had begun to sparkle. "I'm not Father Christmas; I work hard for my money, and when I spend it I want to be sure I get good value in return. How do I know that you would be good value, Miss Would-Be-Event-Rider?"

"Oh, Mr Hissey, I *would* be," I assured him. "I work hard and I would train hard. I *wouldn't* let you down; you could ask Hans to give me a reference."

"I could," the Pickle King agreed. "And I most certainly would."

"And the horse is good value," I said eagerly. "It's actually very cheap. It's the right type and the right age, and it's sound in every way because I've had it vetted. It's exactly the horse for the job, you could go and see it for yourself."

"Oh, I would," he said. "Make no mistake about it."

"It would be a good investment," I urged him. "Even if it didn't make the grade, you would still come out with a profit at the end of the exercise. You couldn't possibly lose money."

"Unless it broke its neck," he said.

"There is such a thing as insurance," I pointed out.

"An insurance premium on an event horse is very costly," he said solemnly.

"You wouldn't have to pay the running costs," I told him. "I can keep a horse in the yard where I work; it's a condition of the job."

"You must be earning a very good wage," the Pickle King said, "to be confident that you can afford the upkeep of an event horse; the training, the transportation, the entry fees, not to mention the best quality food, the supplements, the shoeing, the saddlery, the veterinary charges."

There was nothing I could say to this. The Pickle King leaned back in his chair and stuck his thumbs into the pockets of his jolly yellow waistcoat. He regarded me in amusement. He knew perfectly well that I wasn't earning a bean. Everyone who hunted in the Midvale and Westbury country knew the Fanes.

"Now, in my yard," he observed in an innocent tone, "I do pay extremely good wages. I pay more than the NAG rate for the job; and as a concession, there happens to be a vacant stable, with keep, for a horse that might, just might, you understand, be an eventer."

"Mr Hissey," I said, appalled. "That's bribery!"

"No, no," the Pickle King said comfortably. "It's known as setting a sprat to catch a mackerel."

"But I already have a job," I said. "I'm not sure that I want to leave. At least," I added, "not yet."

"The trouble with horse-mad little girls," the Pickle King said sternly, "is that they don't realize, don't *want* to realize, that they are being exploited. If I worked my pickling ladies the hours that you are expected to work, and paid them the rate you are getting, I would have the union down on me like a ton of bricks."

"Mr Hissey," I said. "Are you saying that if I take your job, you will buy the bay gelding?"

"The problem is," he continued, "that in the horse world, apart from in the racing sector, there is no nationally supervised training scheme, just a rather fragmented examination system . . ."

"Mr Hissey," I interrupted. "Am I right? Is that what you are saying?"

". . . Which is, in any case, undersubsidized, oversubscribed, and leans rather too heavily towards the art of instruction; therefore a really good well-trained groom, like a good nose, is a rare find." He rocked back in his chair towards the desk and gave me an angelic smile. "Are you a really good, well-trained groom, Miss Would-Be-Event-Rider?"

"Yes," I said, wanting to be truthful. "I believe I am."

"Then what I am saying," the Pickle King said, "is that in all propositions laid before a man of business,

138

there must be a raison d'être, an inducement, a benefit."

"Mr Hissey," I said. "I think you are a snake in the grass."

Unabashed, he beamed at me over the piles of orange powder. "I dislike conducting interviews," he continued. "It would give me great pleasure to tear up the advertisement I was about to insert in *Horse and Hound*, to be spared the agony of sorting through an avalanche of unsuitable applicants. Consequently, if you will consider my job, in return, I will consider the bay gelding. Now, Miss Would-Be-Event-Rider, do we have a bargain?"

"Yes, Mr Hissey," I said. "We do."

14

A Very Old Mare

The old bay mare was flat out in her stable and I couldn't get her up. I was dressed for hunting, but I couldn't leave her because I knew in my bones that she was going to die. It was Doreen's half-term, and she stood in the doorway, wide-eyed. Her white face was almost transparent with dismay.

"Go and find Nigella," I said. "Tell her the old bay mare is worse; that I am going to stay behind, and that you are to take the blue roan instead of me."

"Oh, I *can't*," Doreen moaned. "The Fanes won't like it."

The old bay mare's eyes had sunk and her breathing was fast and shallow. I had heaped rugs on top of her but her ears, when I felt them, were like wet leather gloves left out in a frost.

"The Fanes will have to lump it," I said. "I can't go off and leave her like this."

"What did you say?" Henrietta exclaimed, appearing at the door with her plaiting box under her arm. "Can't go? Of course you can go. It isn't as if you can do anything for her, after all. She's pretty far gone already; she won't notice if you are here or not."

"I'm going to stay," I said. "I've called the vet."

"I thought we had decided not to call the vet," Henrietta said peevishly. "You know he won't be able to do anything, and he'll charge us the earth just for the visit."

"I've called him anyway," I said. "There might be a chance. Doreen will take the blue roan."

"Oh, I don't *know*," Doreen wailed. "I've never ridden it before."

"You see," Henrietta said. "She won't. She's hopeless."

"Ow," Doreen squeaked, offended. "I'm *not*."

"Then go and get your hunting clothes," I said crossly. "This minute."

Doreen went off, looking uncertain. The old bay mare managed a tremulous sigh, although she was really past caring.

"If she falls off . . ." Henrietta warned. "If she damages the horse . . ."

"She won't fall off, and she won't damage the horse," I said, "because you will be there to see that she doesn't."

"Hrmm," Henrietta said, and she went off to change with a disgruntled air.

The Fanes were not able to use their side-saddles on the Thunder and Lightning liveries for fear of causing sore backs and confusion over the aids, so they were forced to ride astride. I had offered them the loan of the stretch jodhpurs I wore for exercising, but they had refused. When they appeared in the yard, ready to mount, I could see why. Amongst the jumble offerings they had discovered several pairs of ex-cavalry elephant-ear breeches in a vibrant shade of ginger, and appropriated them for their own use. No self-respecting rider would have dreamed of wearing them, but the Fanes thought them delightful.

"Wait until you see my other pair," Henrietta said gleefully. "In black and white houndstooth check."

Doreen, legged up into the blue roan's beautiful *Stübben* saddle, whispered that she couldn't wait.

"There are some smaller sizes," Nigella said benevolently. "We should sort out a pair for Doreen."

Doreen followed them out of the yard, looking troubled.

When the vet came I asked him if there was any hope. He examined the old bay mare and he took her temperature and he listened to her failing heartbeat.

"No," he said. "I'm afraid there's no hope at all. She's a very old mare and there would be no point in trying to prolong her life. It wouldn't be fair; in fact, it would be unkind to try. It's far better to just let her slip quietly away; she isn't in any pain."

He helped me to heap the blankets back on to her. "You mustn't be too sad," he said. "After all, it's quite a privilege these days, for a horse to be allowed to die of old age."

Outside in the yard, he asked if I had bought the bay gelding. I told him about my financial position and about Felix Hissey's offer, and that I had six days in which to make up my mind.

"You'll go to Hissey's place, of course," he assumed. "It's exactly what you want; a well-paid job and a chance to event. There's no decision to make, as far as I can see."

"It seems that there isn't," I said. "In fact I've already told Felix Hissey that I'm willing to take his job. He's going to see the bay gelding tomorrow. It all rather hinges on whether he likes it or not."

The vet patted my shoulder. "He can't help but

like it," he said. "It's a grand horse." He left me with two bills, fifteen pounds for vetting the bay gelding, and an eight pound call-out fee for the old bay mare. I knew Henrietta would be furious when she saw it.

I was prepared for a solitary vigil with the old bay mare, but not long after the sound of the vet's car had died away Lady Jennifer appeared with two mugs of coffee on a tin tray. They were accompanied by the last of the biscuits and a new packet of raw cane sugar. I didn't need to be told where the latter had come from. Lady Jennifer had been to lunch with my father the previous day; already he was making his influence felt.

Lady Jennifer settled herself down on the straw and gently lifted the old bay mare's head into her faded tweed lap. And whilst we waited, she told me about her youth and the many hunters she had owned, and how, although never beautiful, Little Legend had once been the envy of the country because of her speed and her courage. And as she related all this, her eyes grew damp, and she wiped tears off the old bay mare's nose with a crumpled paper tissue.

"I mustn't be sentimental," she sniffed. "It's so *terribly* silly of me, and it doesn't help at all."

When the old bay mare finally stopped breathing with a single long, shuddering rasp, Lady Jennifer closed her eyelids over her sunken eyes as gently and carefully as if she had been a human and lifted the lifeless head from her lap; then she went out of the stable to summon the flesh waggon.

I saddled up the bad-tempered chestnut and went out for a ride so that I shouldn't have to witness the indignity of the old bay mare's departure. I knew that it really made no difference at all what happened to her once she was dead, but I was haunted by something William had said when Lady Jennifer and I had returned the young entry to the kennels on the day of my arrival; that all the hirelings together wouldn't feed hounds for more than a week. Well, the old bay mare had been fatter when she died than she had been for a long time; she wouldn't disgrace us now. The sheer awfulness of it brought on a few more tears before I managed to pull myself together, and turned the bad-tempered chestnut for home.

Henrietta and Nigella received the news with regret unclouded by any hint of sentimentality or remorse and soon fell to relating in tones of high excitement the happenings of the day; describing in glowing terms the impeccable behaviour and the general excellence of the Thunder and Lightning liveries. They had been particularly impressed by the blue roan, who, "even with a fool like Doreen in the saddle", had been in the first flight to the end.

They were just contemplating the alarming possibility of letting the liveries out as hirelings when their owners were otherwise engaged, when there was a determined thumping at the front door. I went to answer it.

It was William. He stood in the portico, shuffling his feet and looking as if he would vastly prefer to be somewhere else. He was sorry to have made such a row, he said, but he had knocked a couple of times before and nobody had heard. I said it was perfectly all right and would he like to come in.

"No," he said awkwardly. "I won't come in, if

that's all right with you. It's very kind of you to ask, but I'd prefer not."

I wondered if he had come to see Henrietta, and had lost his nerve, or if he was the bearer of a message from Forster who had not spoken to me since the incident in the lane, or if it was the lingering odour of B.O. and mothballs that had caused him to turn red to the gills with embarrassment.

But it was none of these things.

"We were sorry about the old mare," he said. "She's been a good horse in her time. We thought you might like to have these." He pushed a brown paper bag into my hands and made off down the steps before I could even say thank you.

Inside the bag, scrubbed and burnished, were the old bay mare's shoes.

15

A Good Day's Hunting

"Whatever 'The Lads' happen to be like," Henrietta said, "we must make sure that they enjoy themselves. Our livelihood depends upon it."

We all agreed that we would do our best, but on Thursday morning it was bitterly cold and raining hard.

"They won't come," Nigella decided. "They are sure to be fair weather riders. I wouldn't send my worst enemy hunting on a day like this." But we plaited up just in case, and at ten fifteen a white Mercedes drew into the yard.

"The Lads" were a lot smaller, younger and punier than they had looked on the television, but they were friendly and optimistic and they were looking forward to their day with the Hunt, rain or no rain.

"Heavens," Nigella exclaimed when she was introduced to them. "I thought you were bald!"

Johnny Jones leaned towards her and unpeeled one of his sideburns. "We are," he said. "This is a wig."

"Oh, please," Nigella said, dismayed. "Don't take it off."

"It's only 'is 'ead," Sammy Pike said reassuringly. "It ain't indecent exposure."

When "The Lads" were introduced to their horses, they all wanted the blue roan. Things got so heated that Nigella was forced to take charge and allocate the horses size by size. So Johnny Jones got the blue roan because he was the smallest and puniest, Solly Chell got the chestnut, and Sammy Pike, because he was the tallest, got the smallest horse, which was the bay.

Whilst "The Lads" changed into their hunting clothes we tacked up their horses and loaded them into the horsebox and as soon as we had pointed them in the direction of the meet, we began to fly round getting ourselves and our own horses ready. We knew it was essential that we turned out; we had to keep an eye on our livelihood. It was still pouring with rain.

It was not a day on which to feel responsible for someone else's enjoyment. The Fanes and I missed the meet because we had to hack there, but it didn't matter, the first two coverts were blank anyway. The weather had worsened by the time we arrived at the third draw, a wind-lashed thicket perched on the top of a hill and exposed to the full force of the elements. There was a vicious east wind coming off the sea which gave an icy edge to the squalling rain. Henrietta said we were standing on the highest part of Suffolk and that there was nothing on the same level between us and Russia. I didn't know if this was true or not, but it certainly felt like it, and I decided that this day would be the end, the absolute finish, of the Thunder and Lightning liveries.

"The Lads" stood in a miserable huddle with their coat collars up and their backs to the battering wind. Their faces were blue, their expensive hunting clothes were soaked, and water dribbled off their hats and their horses' chins. Nigella and I placed ourselves a little way off and shivered. I could feel water beginning to seep down my neck and my thighs were numb. The mare-who-sometimes-slipped-a-stifle and the bad-tempered chestnut stood with wretchedly bowed heads, whilst Henrietta and the black horse squelched ceaselessly up and down. It was utterly dreadful. Then, like a miracle, we heard the Gone Away.

In the flurry of the first few minutes, struggling to regain our circulation, we could see that "The Lads" were no horsemen. They sat with loose reins and flapping legs and they had no idea how to control their horses at all. It was clear that this would lead to disaster because the country was treacherous. The stubble fields of the autumn were almost all gone, replaced by wide acres of deep, sticky plough criss-crossed by greasy tracks studded with loose flints. The yawning banked ditches which divided the land were not improved by the rain, their sides were slimy with exposed clay, and their dug out gullies gushed with yellow water.

As the Field dived after the Master, the Fanes and I held back, ready to pick up the pieces of our livelihood. We were certain that they would come to grief; it wasn't a day, or a country, for riders without experience.

"They'll be killed," Henrietta gasped in a despairing voice. She sat down hard and fought the black horse gamely with slippery reins, her sodden apron flapping against his ribs. "Think of their insurance company! Think of our seventy-five pounds a week!"

But it was the horses I was thinking about, forseeing sprains and strains and broken limbs, and at the third ditch we came upon the blue roan, upside down and stuck fast, kicking like a turtle.

"Oh, glory," Nigella moaned. "Where's Johnny Jones?"

We scanned the grey and buffeted headland, expecting to see him lying injured, but Johnny Jones was not in sight. Then, from the depths of the ditch, we heard an inarticulate noise.

"He's here!" Henrietta shouted. "He's under the horse!" Panic-stricken, she leapt off the black horse, slid down the side of the ditch, and began to tug helplessly at the blue roan's reins. The tail end of the Field, near blinded by the rain, flew past, splattering her with mud.

"No! No!" Nigella cried. "You'll never move her like that! We shall have to use stirrup leathers!"

I dragged the leathers off the mare-who-sometimes-slipped-a-stifle's saddle and yanked off the irons. As I threw the leathers to Nigella, the black horse, unable to bear the sight of the departing hunt without protest stood on his hind legs, dragging the bunch of slippery reins from my grasp. I dived for his head and in an instant the mare-who-sometimes-slipped-a-stifle and the bad-tempered chestnut realized that they were free and trotted off smartly in the wake of the tail-enders.

"Let them go!" Henrietta yelled, as I lifted my foot to the black horse's stirrup to be after them. "Don't leave us! Johnny Jones may be injured; you may have to ride for help!"

Somehow the Fanes managed to get the leathers under the blue roan's withers whilst I held on to the black horse who plunged about like something demented.

"Now," Henrietta commanded, her face shining

with rain and red with exertion, and her habit trailing in the mud. "PULL!"

They pulled. The blue roan pressed her head forward and flailed her legs mightily. She rolled over on to her side. Then, with a heave and a grunt, she was up the bank and standing safely on the headland. Johnny Jones lay flattened into the mud at the bottom of the ditch, saved by the hollow of the gully. He sat up and poured water out of his boots. "If this is hunting in Suffolk," he said, "you can keep it."

"Nonsense," Henrietta said briskly. "You're having a lovely time." She helped him up the bank and legged him back on to the blue roan.

A woman in a bowler hat rode up to us, leading a chestnut horse. "Excuse me," she said. "Is this one of yours?"

"No," Nigella said firmly, wringing ditch water out of the bottom of her apron. "It isn't," and then, "Wait a moment," she said. "I believe it is." It wasn't the bad-tempered chestnut, it was the chestnut livery.

"All this isn't really happening," said Henrietta grimly, as she took hold of the black horse's rein as a preliminary to the search for Solly Chell. "It's just a nightmare. I shall wake up in a minute."

I threaded the irons on to the leathers, put them over my shoulders, and mounted the chestnut livery. Johnny Jones was a speck in the distance.

"What about me," Nigella enquired. "I haven't got a horse." Henrietta legged her up behind me on the chestnut livery and we set off along the headland. The black horse progressed across the plough in a series of giant leaps and the chestnut livery cantered at a sedate pace with his double burden. The wind whipped our clothes and slashed our faces with icy rain. "I think this day might turn out to be the worst of my life," said Nigella.

Two fields on we came upon Sammy Pike and the bay horse wandering up and down a banked ditch in a dazed manner, looking for a way to cross. Across his cheekbone there was a bloody gash and a rapidly gathering bruise. He told us that he had been galloping behind someone when their horse had thrown up a flint.

"Well, if you must gallop on someone's tail," Henrietta said. "Remember to keep your head down."

Nigella wondered if the cut should have a stitch but Sammy Pike said no fear.

"But you'll have a scar," Nigella said anxiously.

"Yeah," Sammy Pike said, pleased. "I've always wanted a scar on me face."

"Heavens," Nigella said in a low voice. "There's no way of understanding some people."

Henrietta was demonstrating to Sammy Pike the correct way to approach the banked ditch. "When it's dry you have a choice between scrambling down it, or flying it. But when it's wet there's no choice, you simply have to fly it. You must approach it at a controlled gallop because you need plenty of impulsion to get up the bank and to take you over the top. If you approach it too slowly, your horse will never make it, and if his back legs slip back into the ditch, throw yourself clear so that he doesn't roll on top of you. Come on, I'll give you a lead."

She trotted the black horse away from the ditch and turned him towards it. "And don't ride on my tail," she shouted to Sammy Pike, "because if I don't make it, you will land on top of me!"

The black horse galloped at the ditch like the old hand he was, leapt up the bank and flew over the top with his tail and Henrietta's hair, which had escaped from its coil, streaming out behind them. Sammy Pike, his eyes lit with excitement, urged the bay after them. He had no idea of how to control a horse at a gallop with his slack seat and flapping arms, but the bay bounded up the bank and flung itself heroically across the gap, landing with several yards to spare.

"I hope you realize what a super horse that is," Henrietta said severely, as she dispatched him in the approximate direction of the hunt.

Nigella and I and the chestnut livery made our way along the top of the bank until we came to a tractor crossing. We traversed the headland of a vast plough field and breasted a long rise of stubble without any sign of Solly Chell or the bad-tempered chestnut, but when we reached the top of the rise, we saw a small crowd gathered round a horse in the lane below.

A woman with a child on a leading rein trotted up the rise towards us. "I wouldn't go any nearer unless you must," she called. "It's broken a leg. They've sent for the humane killer." She pointed to a small white van bucketing across the lower stubble towards the lane.

"Henrietta," Nigella said in a horrified voice. "The horse in the lane looks like our bay mare!"

Henrietta's face stiffened. She lifted her whip hand. The black horse shot forward and flew helter-skelter down the rise. He stretched out his neck and raced the white van towards the knot of people in the lane.

The chestnut livery, sensing the urgency of the situation, leapt after him. He galloped down the rise as fast as his legs would carry him and Nigella and I clung on grimly, slipping further and further sideways. "Don't shoot the mare! Don't shoot her!" Nigella screamed. "She hasn't broken a leg, she's just slipped a stifle!"

With a determined effort of willpower, we managed to stay on the chestnut livery until we saw that Henrietta had arrived in the lane, seconds before the Terrier Man climbed out of the van with the killer in his hands.

"Don't you dare shoot this mare," she cried dramatically. "She's ours!"

Nigella and I hit the stubble together, still clutching each other like Siamese twins. The onlookers gasped, unused to such goings-on, but the Terrier Man was unimpressed.

"She ain't no good to you now, Miss," he said dismally to Henrietta. "Her leg's broke."

Nigella and I picked ourselves up from the stubble. The bay mare's hind leg hung uselessly from her hip. When she moved, she hopped on three legs. I had never seen a slipped stifle, but it looked broken to me.

"You can see for y'self," the Terrier Man said gloomily. "It's definitely broke."

"Nonsense," Henrietta said. "Put that gun away. You know you're not supposed to shoot any animal without a veterinary opinion."

"I don't need a vet to tell me its leg's broke," the Terrier Man said stubbornly.

Nigella untangled herself from the stirrup leathers and picked up the mud-caked end of her apron. She walked into the lane and without a word, took the bay mare by the reins and began to lead her away. The mare hopped obligingly after her. By the time they had covered a hundred yards, she was already putting the injured leg to the ground, although she was still hopelessly lame.

"There you are," Henrietta said in a satisfied voice. "I told you it wasn't broken." She turned the black horse and rode off down the lane after Nigella.

The Terrier Man shrugged his shoulders and plodded morosely back to his van where his charges could be heard yapping and scrabbling in their cages. The crowd of foot-followers began to break up, and I mounted the chestnut livery and followed the Fanes, thinking that I would probably never experience anything like this if I went to work for Felix Hissey, and wondering if I should be glad or sorry.

When we arrived at the Thunder and Lightning horsebox, we found Johnny Jones and Sammy Pike ensconced cheerfully in the cab with a half empty bottle of Scotch between them. Far from having had a disastrous day, they had thoroughly enjoyed it and couldn't wait to come out again. We all accepted a drink, being in need of something to revive us, and got a bit giggly, especially when we opened the back of the box to hospitalize the bay mare, and saw the liveries' legs had been bandaged so loosely that they had concertina'd round their ankles like schoolboys' socks. By the time we had rebandaged the horses, Nigella had gone into one of her flat spins and was being eaten up with anxiety over drink and driving and the safety of the horses, whereupon Johnny

Jones assured her that it was perfectly all right because Solly Chell did all the driving and he never touched a drop. This only made matters worse because Nigella reminded us that for all we knew, Solly Chell might be lying unconscious, half-drowned in a ditch somewhere, not only that, but we were a horse short, and what did we intend to do about it. Didn't we realize that it was getting dark, and shouldn't somebody call the police . . .

The situation was finally saved by the sound of hoof beats on the lane which heralded the arrival of Solly Chell mounted on the bad-tempered chestnut, still bursting with the exhilaration of the chase. He had fallen from his horse when it had veered away from a refuser at a ditch, and he had captured the bad-tempered chestnut as it had trotted by. He had no idea that he had started out on one horse and ended the day on another.

16

King in a Pickle

Nelson and I toiled up the immaculate pea-gravelled drive lined with reproduction street lamps, towards Winter Place. I had tried to telephone Felix Hissey at the factory but I had been unable to speak to him; he was at home, they had said, indisposed.

I needed to see him because he hadn't been out hunting the previous day, and I wouldn't see him at the Saturday meet because I wasn't going; there wasn't a horse for me to ride. In a week we had lost the old bay mare, the mare-who-sometimes-slipped-a-stifle was out of action, probably for the rest of the season, and The Comet had been declared unsafe. This left us with only three hunters, and we had Mr McLoughlin to mount. The season had only just begun and already we were short of horses.

Winter Place was a large, four square neo-Georgian house built of red Suffolk brick with a lot of long white-painted windows. It was very smart and very silent. Nelson and I crunched our way round the back and into the stable yard. There were four garages and three loose boxes. I wondered how much I would enjoy working in this tiny, spotless yard, and if I would be lonely. Felix Hissey's two cobby hunters regarded us with astonishment; they didn't seem accustomed to visitors at Winter Place.

I put Nelson in the empty stable and stroked the noses of the cobs. All through my school years, at the training centre, and even at the Fanes', I had worked with people of my own age. I didn't know solitude and I was bothered by it. I was even more bothered when I met the cross, grey-haired house-keeper, who set her mouth in a grim line and said she would ask if Mr Hissey was prepared to see me.

I told myself firmly that the bay gelding would make up for all this and I followed the grim house-keeper through the hall lined with hunting prints, into a small room lined with books. Felix Hissey was lying in an armchair with his foot propped up in front of him. It was encased in plaster of Paris from the knee downwards.

The Pickle King glowered.

"Oh no," I said weakly. "You *didn't* . . ."

"You don't think, Miss Would-Be-Event-Rider," he snapped, "that I would contemplate the purchase of a horse I hadn't ridden?"

"I don't know," I said helplessly. "It didn't occur to me."

"It didn't occur to you to warn me that it had a buck like a jerboa either," the Pickle King expostulated.

I wasn't sure what a jerboa was, but I felt the bay gelding slip irretrievably from my grasp. "Mr Hissey," I said. "I'm terribly sorry."

"I might have expected it from that lugubrious fool, Harry Sabin," he said in disgust. "But not from you, Miss Would-Be-Event-Rider, I expected better things from you."

"Mr Hissey," I said, ashamed, "what can I say?"

"You can start by saying when you intend to begin work in the yard," he said. "I can't do a thing with this damned leg – which, I might add, Miss Would-Be-Event-Rider, could have been avoided if you had seen fit to give me prior warning."

I couldn't argue. It was true that I had been negligent, and because of it I had lost the bay gelding; and even without the bay gelding I would have to come to Winter Place. It was my penance. "I expect I could leave the Fanes on a fortnight's notice," I said.

"And how am I expected to look after my horses during this fortnight?" the Pickle King enquired peevishly. "With this leg, and without a groom?"

"I'll come twice a day," I said humbly. "I'll cut out their corn and turn them out in the daytime in their New Zealand rugs. I'll give them two small soft feeds morning and night and plenty of hay. I shall have to let them down, there's no point in trying to keep them fit. You won't be riding again for at least six weeks."

"Six weeks," the Pickle King said resentfully. "The season will be over!"

"It won't," I assured him. "You will be hunting again before Christmas."

"Christmas," he said in an explosive tone. "Pah!" He lapsed into a miserable silence.

"Mr Hissey," I said. "Would you like me to see to the horses before I go?" It seemed the least that I could do.

"Yes," he said grudgingly. "Thank you . . . and get Mrs Short to show you the flat . . . you'll get forty pounds a week all found and the use of the pick-up . . . one day a week off in half days during the hunting season and two full months off with pay in the summer . . ."

"Thank you," I said. "You're very generous." I had never felt more unhappy in the whole of my life.

"Oh," he added. "And there's the money." He pointed to a fat manilla envelope on the desk.

"Money?" I said stupidly. "What money?"

"The money for Harry Sabin's bay gelding," he said. "I've never ridden a better horse in my life."

"Nigella," I said. "I'm leaving in a fortnight."

Nigella looked up from the *Horse and Rider* she was reading. "Oh *Elaine*," she sighed. "Not again!"

"I mean it this time," I said. "I've written out my notice. I've got another job." I told her about Felix Hissey and the bay gelding.

"I can't believe it," she said. "How could you do this to us? We thought you were happy here."

"I have been," I said. "I honestly have been. I feel terrible about it; but I have my future to think of, and this is the only way."

"Why didn't you talk to us about it?" she wondered. "You didn't mention the bay gelding; why didn't you tell us? Why did it have to be a secret?"

"If I had told you," I said. "If we had discussed it, you couldn't have done anything, and Henrietta . . . well, Henrietta would have interfered."

"Yes," Nigella agreed. "She would." We fell silent, thinking about Henrietta. "I shall have to tell her," she decided. "She won't like it, and I expect she will make your last two weeks as difficult as possible, but I can't not tell her, can I?"

"No," I said. "You can't."

"I had hoped," Nigella said, getting up from the table, "that you would stay with us for years and years." She went out of the door rather quickly, but not before I had seen that her eyes were bright with tears.

"Elaine," Lady Jennifer said. "As you are not hunting tomorrow, could you *possibly* help me with the jumble sale?"

"Oh dear," I said. "Must I?" I had planned to collect the bay gelding and take him to Winter Place; but Lady Jennifer was not to be put off.

"I'm so *frightfully* short of helpers," she sighed. "I just don't know *how* I shall manage; and it isn't as if I would need you all day, it doesn't begin until two o'clock."

I sighed inwardly. I knew it would take me all morning to finish my work in the stables, and added to that I had to get to Winter Place to look after the cobs as well. If I helped Lady Jennifer with her awful jumble sale, I would have to put off collecting the bay gelding until Sunday. It was a nuisance, but I was fond of Lady Jennifer and I didn't want to refuse.

"Of course I'll help," I said. "I'll be delighted."

Mucking out alone in the deserted yard when everyone had left for the Saturday meet I told myself that I should be feeling elated, that surely I must be one of the luckiest people alive. At last I had landed a good job with a fair living wage and regular time off; I had never received a penny from the Fanes, and they still owed me the pound I had loaned them in the underground car park. I hadn't had a day off either, in the month I had worked for them. Was it only a month? It seemed longer than that.

I told myself that not only had I landed a good

job, but that I also had the bay gelding, I had the potential event horse I had dreamed of; and yet I still couldn't shake off a feeling of blankness; there was a sort of hollow void where the elation should have been. I wondered if perhaps now that it had actually come to it, I was getting cold feet about the task ahead, if it was nerves that were anaesthetizing the bit of me that should have been bursting with joy. Perhaps I should have stayed with Hans Gelderhol when he had offered to take me on in his yard. He would have given me a few pounds a week and I could have become one of his acolytes. The acolytes had a few doubtful privileges, but sponsored event horses were not among them. Hans Gelderhol had said that I was "promising", but what did that mean? It meant that I had a lot to learn, and professional training was expensive; everything to do with eventing was expensive; eventing was a rich person's sport, whichever way you looked at it. Well, thank heavens for Felix Hissey. Felix Hissey was a rich man. I thought of Felix Hissey sitting with his foot up, whilst everyone else was at the Saturday meet, and I was ashamed.

Preoccupied with all this, I led The Comet out in his New Zealand rug and loosed him into the park. There was a Harrods van in the drive. I wondered if Lady Jennifer knew it was there and I decided that she did, because the front door was standing open.

I lit the boiler in the feed room and put in the barley and the linseed and the water to cook very gently so that it would be ready to make into a mash when the horses came in from hunting. I filled hay nets and water buckets, I tidied the tack room and I swept the yard and I wondered why I felt flattened.

Did everyone who suddenly found themselves in possession of everything they had ever wanted feel flattened? I didn't know. I went to get changed for the jumble sale.

On our way to the village hall, we met Henrietta, riding home on the black horse. It was only half past one, so I knew that something must be wrong.

"He's a bit lame," she explained. "So I thought I had better bring him back."

My heart sank. The horses were going down like ninepins. Now there were only two hirelings left out of six, and one of those had only one eye. I couldn't imagine how the Fanes were going to get through the season. I jumped out of the shooting brake to look at the black horse's legs. I knew it couldn't be thrush causing the lameness because his feet were now completely clean and sound.

Henrietta had said nothing at all about my notice and I had found this hard to understand because I had expected a scene. "There's really no need to fuss," she said in an irritated tone, as I ran my hands down his legs and felt his hooves for heat. "He's probably just stepped on a flint or something. I'll look at him properly when I get him home."

"I can't find anything wrong with him," I said, puzzled. "If you could trot him up the lane for a little way, I might be able to see where the trouble is."

"Elaine!" Lady Jennifer shrilled anxiously. "We must not delay a *moment* longer, or we shall be *terribly* late!"

"You'd better go," Henrietta said hastily.

I jumped back into the shooting brake, still watching the black horse for any clue to his unsoundness. Henrietta rode him towards the Hall. He broke into an anxious trot, impatient for his stable and his supper. He trotted remarkably well for a lame horse.

Outside the village hall, a queue of determined looking women had formed. When the doors were opened they raced for the stalls and everything seemed to fly into the air at once. I had no idea that a jumble sale was such hard work. We worked flat out all afternoon and our tins of silver overflowed.

"You won't be expected to lift a *finger* in the stables this evening," Lady Jennifer promised. "The girls will do everything. You look absolutely *exhausted*. I can't begin to tell you what a *marvellous* help you have been."

At the end of the sale, when Lady Jennifer had collected all the tins and was seated at a trestle table counting the piles of silver, surrounded by a bevy of jubilant ladies, I wandered outside to get some fresh air. It was beginning to get dark as I walked slowly down to the village green, nursing my inexplicable emptiness. I stood on the grass remembering the morning of the opening meet, and like an echo, I heard the sound of the hunt returning to the kennels.

I moved into the shadow of a tree and I watched them pass by in the fading light. The horses clopped past the shadowy cottages on lengthened reins and hounds ambled beside them with lowered sterns. The young entry must have been there, although I wouldn't have known which they were, Forster was there, and William, and the Huntsman, with the horn tucked between the buttons of his coat. And following them home came Brenda on her pink-nosed cob, and Doreen on her pony, and further behind still came Nigella on Nelson and Mr McLoughlin on the bad-tempered chestnut. They all looked very contented and companionable, and the lights pricked out from the cottages around the green, and nobody saw me, under the tree.

17

Another Legend

"Harry!" I called. "Harry Sabin! Are you there?" The dirt yard was deserted. There was nobody tinkering with the cattle waggon. I wondered if I was too early, if Harry Sabin was still in bed. I had set off at six thirty; before anyone at the Hall had been up, in order to feed and muck out the cobs, and make the spare box ready for the bay gelding at Winter Place. Then, with the manilla envelope in my pocket, I had driven the shooting brake to Harry Sabin's yard, hoping to ride the bay gelding to his new home, and still be back at the Hall in time to help with morning stables. I shouted again.

This time the door of the scruffy patch-roofed cottage opened and Harry Sabin shuffled out in his carpet slippers.

"Harry," I said. "I'm sorry to be so early, but I've brought you the money."

"Now, young lady," he said cautiously, rubbing his unshaven chin. "Which money is that?"

"You know perfectly well," I said. "It's the money for the bay gelding. You wanted it in cash. Before Monday."

"Ah," he said in an uncomfortable tone. "The bay gelding."

"Harry," I said. "The bay gelding is *here*?" Some part of my insides tied themselves into a nasty little knot. The bay gelding wasn't in the stable with the

165

slip rail because it was now occupied by a big grey horse. Neither had he been visible in the top field with the dealer's stock. I pulled the manilla envelope out of my pocket and my heart began to beat heavily under my jersey. "We made a bargain, Harry," I said. "Fifteen hundred pounds in cash. You said you would give me until Monday. You *promised*."

"Well now," Harry Sabin said, embarrassed. "That's a little bit difficult, that is."

"What's difficult about it, Harry," I asked. "Where is the bay gelding?"

Harry Sabin looked down at his greasy carpet slippers. He stuck his hands into the pockets of his warehouse coat. He shrugged his wiry shoulders and he looked at me with his foxy brown eyes. "That's a little hard to say, Miss," he admitted.

"Oh, Harry," I said, agonized. "You've sold him, haven't you? After we had made a bargain; after you had given me time to find the money!" I couldn't believe he could have done such a thing. "Oh, *Harry*," I groaned. "And it isn't even *Monday* yet!"

"I never thought you'd get the money," he muttered. "And that's the truth of it."

"But Felix Hissey put up the money," I said in despair. "Felix Hissey came to try him. He was going to be my sponsor, surely you *knew*!"

"Felix Hissey never said nothing to me," Harry Sabin said. "Neither did you for that matter, and Felix Hissey got his leg broke. That didn't look as if he'd be interested after that. That didn't look promising."

"Where did you sell him to?" I demanded. "Who bought him?" I had wild ideas of going after them, trying to buy him back.

166

"I didn't ask no questions," Harry Sabin said. "The waggon had London plates on it."

I could see it was no use. "How much did they give you?" I asked him bitterly. "As a matter of interest, how much did they pay?"

"Sixteen hundred," he said, adding in a disparaging tone, "That was a better offer than yours, anyhow."

It seemed incredibly, unbelievably unjust that I should have lost the bay gelding for a hundred pounds; when a hundred pounds, or two or even three, would have been nothing, absolutely nothing, to Felix Hissey.

"Did they pay you in cash?" I said, catching at a straw. If they hadn't, I wondered if I might be able to trace them through their bank.

"I told you," Harry Sabin said sullenly. "I don't take no cheques."

It was hopeless. I walked slowly back across the yard to the shooting brake. I was completely stunned. Numb. I might have driven away without another word, but as I passed the ramshackle building, the grey horse nickered to me and I recognized The Comet's familiar greeting. The Comet!

"Harry!" I yelled. "What the devil is The Comet doing in your stable?"

"He's going to Warners," he said defensively. "Instead of the bay gelding."

"Oh no," I shouted. "He is NOT!" Suddenly, I could hardly see straight. I turned round on Harry Sabin and pushed him aside. I grabbed the bridle out of the shooting brake and flung away the slip rail. I yanked the bridle on to The Comet, who was so astonished that he had his mouth open even before I got the browband past his nose. I was livid. My anger exploded into flashes of bright, bloody red. I was boiling with anger, and my fury was directed against Harry Sabin; the people who had deprived me of the bay gelding; the Fanes. Everybody. I dragged The Comet out of the stable and vaulted on to his back.

"Harry Sabin," I hissed. "You are a bent, slippery, double-tongued rogue!" I clapped my heels into The Comet's sides and he flew out of the yard in a cloud of dirt. Down the track and out on to the lane The Comet flew, round the corner and across the verge and along the tarmac. Faster and faster went The Comet, but I didn't care. I couldn't have stopped him and I didn't even try. Up the Hall drive The Comet thundered, swerving under the clock arch and skidding to a halt on the cobbles.

Henrietta was crossing the yard with a hay net. "Goodness," she said in a calm voice. "You've brought The Comet back. Whatever for?"

"Whatever for!" I shouted. "*Whatever for*? Because he was going to Warners, that's what *for*!"

"I thought you knew," Henrietta said. "I was sure I had mentioned it." She frowned.

"You can't send a horse like The Comet to a *sale*," I cried. "He's dangerous! He's a bolter! If you declare it, he'll go for meat! If you don't, they'll find out and they'll sue you; then they'll shoot him anyway!"

Henrietta shrugged. "He's no use to us," she said. "What else can we do with him?"

"You can sell him to me," I said furiously. "*I'll* buy him."

Nigella appeared. "Buy The Comet?" she said,

astonished. "Why should you want to buy The Comet?"

"And anyway," Henrietta enquired. "How will you pay?"

This was the last straw. "I'll pay with the wages I should have had from you!" I cried. "With what I should have been paid for sorting out your messy yard! For caring for your crocked up horses! I'll pay for The Comet with the money you owe me!" I howled.

"Will it be enough?" Nigella said cautiously. "You have only been here a month."

"If it isn't enough," I told her furiously. "I shall make it up somehow."

"Since you are buying The Comet," Henrietta said coolly, "he had better stay. Perhaps you should put him in his old stable."

I slid off The Comet. My legs almost gave way as I hit the cobbles; they seemed to be made of jelly. The Comet clopped beside me across the yard. I was trembling all over. I told myself that this was the end. I had had enough of the Fanes. I couldn't stand them for a minute longer; they were driving me insane. I would take The Comet to Winter Place. I would pack my case and I would ride there; The Comet and I would go together. I wouldn't even stay to work my notice; we would go today. This morning. Now.

I opened the door of The Comet's stable. It was already occupied. By Harry Sabin's bay gelding.

My whole world went round and round. I thought I must be going mad. I clutched The Comet for support.

"We knew you would be pleased," Nigella said. "At least, we hoped you would be."

"Although you rather spoiled things," Henrietta said severely. "We didn't expect you to leave so early. There was to have been a proper presentation; with Mummy and Doreen and Brenda; and even Mr McLoughlin was going to come."

I went into the stable. I felt the bay gelding's satiny neck and I touched his mane. It was true. He was real. He was standing in The Comet's stable.

"How . . ." I stuttered. "How . . . did you find the money?"

"Henrietta sold her secretaire," Nigella said. "It was the only way. It was the only thing we had left."

"It was nothing," Henrietta said diffidently. "People don't really have dowries any more. It's a pretty old-fashioned idea."

"But Henrietta," I said weakly. "You *loved* your secretaire."

She shrugged. "It was only a piece of furniture, after all."

Suddenly, it all began to fall into place; the Harrods van, the black horse's invisible lameness, Lady Jennifer insisting that I should help at the jumble sale, the Thunder and Lighʒning horsebox with its London plates; even Harry Sabin must have known.

"You were all in the plot!" I exclaimed. "You all schemed against me!"

"Not against you," Nigella corrected. "*For* you."

"And you schemed as well," Henrietta pointed out. "When it came to getting what you wanted, you schemed more than anybody."

170

I couldn't argue; but the Fanes, through their interference, had put me in a very difficult position.

"I don't want you to think I don't appreciate what you have done," I said, agonized. "But the situation isn't as simple as it looks. I *have* to take Felix Hissey's job, because he has broken a leg and he can't look after his horses. I *promised*!"

"You must do as you wish, of course," Nigella said. "But when Mummy went to see Mr Hissey yesterday morning, he was very understanding. He said that he wouldn't hold you to your side of the bargain if, in return, we agreed to livery his horses free until Christmas."

"And to be perfectly honest," Henrietta said. "It suits us very well, because we are extremely short of horses."

"You don't look all that pleased," Nigella said anxiously. "I hope you don't think we have gone too far. We only did it because we didn't want you to leave. We thought you didn't really want to leave either, that all you really wanted was the bay gelding."

"And now that you've got the bay gelding," Henrietta added with a touch of her customary malice, "perhaps you would be good enough to take The Comet back to Harry Sabin."

"The Comet isn't going back to Harry Sabin," I said heatedly. "He isn't going to Warners!"

"Oh no," Henrietta said. "I forgot. You are going to buy him with the money we owe you."

I stared at her in exasperation. I couldn't tell by her expression whether she was joking or not. I felt upset and disorientated. The Fanes had turned my life upside down and inside out, and I didn't know if they had done it to please me, or to suit their own convenience. I just couldn't work it out. I was dumbfounded.

"Do have a ride," Nigella said. "I'll go and get some tack." She returned with a Thunder and Lightning saddle and bridle and she put them on the bay gelding. "Please notice," she said, as she led him into the yard, "that we've had him shod." His shoes were buffed and polished, curiously bright.

"By a stroke of luck," Henrietta said. "His feet were the same size as the old bay mare's."

I was beginning to feel rather ill. The morning had assumed an unreal quality. Nigella legged me into the saddle and we progressed out of the yard, towards the park.

"We've even given him a name," Henrietta informed me. "We were going to call him Little Legend, after the old bay mare; but as he isn't so little, we decided to call him Another instead."

"Another?" I said. Even in my dazed state of mind, it seemed an odd name for a horse.

"Another Legend," Nigella explained. "It seemed a good name for an eventer. You must admit, it does have a nice ring to it."

I had to admit that it did. The Fanes dragged open the park gate. Then they perched on some sagging rails and looked expectant.

"We can't wait to see you in action," Nigella said admiringly. "He really is magnificent. He's every bit as beautiful as the bay mare. We never thought," she added wonderingly, "that we would ever own an eventer."

"He'll be a marvellous advertisement for the yard," Henrietta said. "We might get more event horses as liveries. He could open up a whole new world for us."

"But he isn't an event horse yet," I pointed out. "He might not even make it. Preparation takes years and it is very expensive. I don't think you realize quite how much it is going to cost. We shall need saddlery and show jumps, we shall need to build a cross country course and mark out a dressage arena. There will be professional training to pay for, and entry fees and transport. An event horse costs a *fortune* to produce." The prospect of being sponsored by the Fanes in their precarious financial position was terrifying. "How shall we possibly afford it?" I asked them. "Without Felix Hissey to pay the bills?"

"Oh, don't worry," Nigella said comfortingly. "I expect we shall manage somehow; we always have."

"But how?" I wanted to know. "*How*?"

"I don't know," she admitted. "But we've got the horse, and that's a start."

"And we've got a business," Henrietta reminded me. "More or less. Such as it is."

"So do ride him for us," Nigella pleaded. "We're just *dying* to see how he goes."

I turned the bay gelding away from the fence and trotted him across the park. I was too stupefied to appreciate how he bent his glossy neck, how the light wind lifted his silky mane, and how he threw out his toes for the sheer joy of being alive. I was too shaken by the traumas of the morning to realize that I didn't have to go to Winter Place, that I had my eventing prospect, and that life with the Fanes would never be dull, never be lonely.

I was too preoccupied with the difficulties that lay

ahead. Hans Gelderhol had prophesied disappointment and frustration, he had warned that I would be bruised and struggling; but he had not promised me failure and I knew that I must cling to that.

Like learning about riding, he had told me, life will be bumpy at first. All these dreams, these fine ideals, they will be damaged; it is in the way of things. If you are ever to succeed, you must be steadfast. You must hold very, very tight to your dream.

Well, it had been bumpy all right, and there would be more and bigger bumps to come. But as I rode across the old turf on Another Legend, owned and sponsored by the Honorable Nigella and Henrietta Fane of Havers Hall, High Suffolk, I was holding very tight to my dream.

The
Jinny
Series

PATRICIA LEITCH

When Jinny Manders rescues Shantih, a chestnut Arab, from a cruel circus, her dreams of owning a horse of her own seem to come true. But Shantih is wild and unrideable.

This is an exciting and moving series of books about a very special relationship between a girl and a magnificent horse.

ARMADA

All these books are available at your local bookshop or newsagent, or can be ordered from the publisher. To order direct from the publishers just tick the title you want and fill in the form below:

Name _____

Address _____

_____

Send to: Collins Childrens Cash Sales
PO Box 11
Falmouth
Cornwall
TR10 9EN

Please enclose a cheque or postal order or debit my Visa/Access –

Credit card no:

Expiry date:

Signature:

– to the value of the cover price plus:

UK: 80p for the first book and 20p per copy for each additional book ordered to a maximum charge of £2.00.

BFPO: 80p for the first book and 20p per copy for each additional book.

Overseas and Eire: £1.50 for the first book, £1.00 for the second book. Thereafter 30p per book.

Armada reserve the right to show new retail prices on covers which may differ from those previously advertised in the text or elswhere.

ARMADA